THE DOCTOR'S DAUGHTER

Whilst the Great War rages in Europe, sleepy Midchester is pitched into a mystery when a man is found dead in an abandoned house. Twenty-four-year-old Peg Bradbourne is well on the way to becoming a spinster detective, but it is a role she is reluctant to accept. When her stepmother also dies in suspicious circumstances, Peg makes a promise to her younger sister, putting aside her own misgivings in order to find out the truth.

SALLY QUILFORD

THE DOCTOR'S DAUGHTER

Complete and Unabridged

LINFORD
Leicester

First published in Great Britain

First Linford Edition
published 2015

A catalogue record for this book is available
from the British Library.

ISBN 978–1–4448–2412–4

Published by
F. A. Thorpe (Publishing)
Anstey, Leicestershire

Set by Words & Graphics Ltd.
Anstey, Leicestershire
Printed and bound in Great Britain by
T. J. International Ltd., Padstow, Cornwall

This book is printed on acid-free paper

Prologue

It was dark when her mother pulled her out of her warm bed. The only light in the room came from the moon. Outside of the bedclothes a chill hung in the air. Mist rose from her mouth as she breathed.

'Come on, Cassie, get up — we have to go!'

'Helen,' she said, her baby-smooth brow furrowing.

'Helen is not coming. Come along, Cassie. We don't have time to wait.' Her mother bundled her into some clothes.

'This isn't my dress,' she said.

'It is your dress, Cassie. Now please hurry up. Your know your father doesn't like to be kept waiting.'

At the bottom of the stairs, he held a candle in one hand and a large leather bag in the other. 'What took you so long?' he said.

'It's her fault. She's slow and stupid.'

'For God's sake . . . '

'You carry her then.'

'Very well.'

He picked the child up and took her out of the house, bundling her into the waiting carriage. 'If we hurry we should make Plymouth in good time,' he said as he climbed up onto the driver's seat.

'Stay down, Cassie,' her mother said, sitting next to her in the back.

'Helen, Helen!' the child cried. She was halted by a sharp slap across her face.

'Helen is not coming,' her mother said, holding her by both shoulders and shaking her violently. 'Get that into your stupid little head.'

'For God's sake,' he groaned again.

She pushed the little girl down into the seat. 'Now sit down and don't make another sound.'

'You're making enough noise for both of you,' he grumbled. 'You'll have to shut up when we're going through the village.' He whipped the horses and they started to move forward, away from the house at the far edge of the town and towards the more populated area. It was not ideal, but

2

it was the only way he could go.

Most of the village of Midchester was asleep as the carriage sped through the marketplace. If anyone heard the carriage, by the time they stumbled out of bed and went to the window, it was long gone.

The carriage carried on out of the village and onto the south-bound road, which would take them through Herefordshire, the Welsh borders and beyond.

1

1916

'We'll have to sell the house.' Veronica Bradbourne looked up briefly from her letter as her stepdaughter entered the breakfast room. 'Really, Margaret, do you have to wear those awful slacks to breakfast? It is hardly lady-like.' Veronica herself wore a mauve dress suit, with a Cossack-style jacket trimmed with fur around the waist and on the sleeves.

Peg was dressed in her late father's white shirt, a mauve floral waistcoat she had made from an old dress she had grown out of, and a pair of corduroy trousers. A mauve handkerchief bound her bright auburn hair. 'I'm going to help out up at Bedlington farm, Veronica. I can hardly dress for a garden party.' She paused for breath. 'I do wish you would stop calling me Margaret.'

She went to the sideboard to fill up her plate, noting how little there was to eat.

The war had finally started to take its toll on the availability of food. She took one slice of bacon, leaving the last for her sister, Sheila.

'Margaret is your name, is it not?' asked her stepmother.

'The last person to call me that was Grandpapa on the day he christened me. Why you insist on using it against all my objections, I don't know.'

'I think you look lovely, Peg,' said ten-year-old Mary, who sat at the table eating porridge.

'That's because you're an angel,' said Peg, blowing her half-sister a kiss.

Sheila Bradbourne bustled into the room. She drew looks of approval from her stepmother on account of being dressed in a pretty tunic with a hobble skirt. 'See?' she addressed Peg.

'It's not difficult to look ladylike, even with a war on,' said Veronica. 'Now where was I?' She frowned. 'Yes, we will have to sell the house.'

'Why?' asked Sheila. She sat at the table and nibbled on a slice of toast. Whereas Peg had inherited the masculine jawline of their father, Sheila had their late mother's heart-shaped face and cupid's-bow lips.

'I left you the last slice of bacon,' said Peg, gesturing to the sideboard.

'I'm quite happy with toast.'

'You're too thin, Sheila. Get some bacon. Or at least put butter on that toast. It'll put hairs on your chest and make up for Norman's lack of them.'

'Norman is man enough for me,' said Sheila. She tried to look annoyed, but failed and stifled a giggle.

'I might as well be talking to myself,' said Veronica. 'Don't you care that we have to sell the house to cover your father's death duties? What do you suppose you will both do? I have to find somewhere smaller for myself and Mary. I'm afraid I can't take you with me.'

'Constable Hounds's old cottage is up for rent,' said Peg. 'We could live there, Sheila.'

'Oh no,' said Sheila. She flicked imaginary dust from her sleeve. 'It's practically falling down.'

'The solicitor is saying that your

father's death duties have to be settled soon,' said Veronica, waving the letter in front of them.

'They're not just Father's death duties,' Peg murmured. 'Unless your dressmaker is part of the Board of the Inland Revenue.'

Veronica pursed her lips. 'Margaret . . . Peg . . . I try to put up with your idiosyncrasies for your late father's sake. But I will not have you blaming me for the situation we are in now.'

'Who else can I blame, Veronica?' asked Peg, pushing her plate away. 'When Mother died, Father had no outstanding debts. Then he married you and somehow we not only have to pay death duties but also a pile of debts.'

'Yes, well I'm sure I would like to listen once again to tales of your mother and what a paragon of virtue she was,' said Veronica, her mouth tightening into a thin line, 'but I'm rather busy at the moment.' She got up and left the room quickly.

Peg mentally kicked herself. Her father had tried to teach her that some arguments were avoidable, yet she was unable to follow his teaching. She put it down to her Irish blood.

'Really, Peg, do you have to be so unkind to her?' asked Sheila. 'She hasn't been a bad stepmother to us.'

'Mama does try very hard,' said Mary, looking forlorn. 'I wish the people I love wouldn't argue. It makes it very hard to know who is right and who is wrong.'

'Oh, I'm sorry, sweetheart.' Peg reached across and took Mary's hand. 'I didn't mean to upset you. You're so sweet, sometimes I forget you're hers.'

'Peg!' Sheila sighed and stood up. 'Don't talk about her mother like that. I have to post a letter to Norman. Do you have anything for Freddie?'

'I'll post it later.'

'I've got a letter for Freddie,' said Mary.

'Hurry up then,' said Sheila. 'I have to be at the school soon. It won't do to be late on my first day.'

'What are we going to do, Sheila?' Peg asked when they were alone.

'I'm going to marry Norman and move

to Sheffield with him.'

'What if he doesn't come back from the front?'

'Can you try and be a bit more tactful?'

Peg waved her hand dismissively. 'Oh you know I don't mean anything by it. I'm just thinking that if we put together the annuities that Great Aunt Bedlington left us, we could live quite well.'

'Peg, you're my sister and I love you. Really I do. Like Father, I'm willing to forgive your idiosyncrasies because I know that deep down your heart is pure. But I am going to be as blunt with you as you are with others. I don't want to share a house with you on Spinsters' Row.' The real name of the street was Station Road, but the relatively cheap housing there led to it being inhabited by elderly gentle-women in distressed circumstances. 'You know yourself,' Sheila continued, 'that once you move into that street, your chances of marrying are nil. I'm twenty-two and you're twenty-four. I intend to marry, even if you don't. I'm going to marry Norman and I am going to have children.'

'Don't you ever want more, Sheila? A career of your own perhaps? You're doing well at the school.'

'Norman thinks a man should be able to keep his wife and children,' Sheila said proudly.

'Don't you ever wish we were back in India?' asked Peg.

'I don't remember it quite as well as you, dear.'

'It was wonderful. So much bigger than this tiny village. Not just the space, but the scope of life there.'

Sheila said sadly, 'I sometimes wonder if Mama would have lived if we'd stayed there. These British winters were so hard on her.'

'Why did Father re-marry so soon?' asked Peg. 'I thought he loved Mama.'

'He did love her, but it's my belief that men don't cope so well alone as widowed women and spinsters do. Whether we like it or not, Peg, he was happy with Veronica.'

'I suppose I should apologise.'

'That would be the correct thing to do.' Sheila looked as if she was about to leave, but she sat down next to her sister and put her arm around her shoulder. 'You know, Peg, you could be very pretty if you tried a bit harder. If you could tidy yourself up and put a nice dress on you could probably find yourself a husband.'

'I am not adorning myself like a Christmas goose in order to ensnare a man. That's the difference between me and you, Sheila. You're terrified of being an old maid, but I'm not. Being alone doesn't frighten me at all.'

'So why do you want me to move in with you?'

'Oh go away and stop asking perfectly reasonable questions. You're the pretty one. You're not supposed to have brains as well.'

Sheila kissed Peg on the cheek and left her sitting alone at the table.

Peg glanced around. 'Being alone is not a problem,' she said out loud. She listened again and was struck by the sound of silence. She managed a few minutes before it became too deafening.

At the top of the stairs, she glanced along the landing and saw Veronica's bedroom door open. Taking a deep breath and promising herself she would not say the wrong thing this time, she went to talk to her stepmother.

Veronica was sitting at the dressing table, putting powder on her face. Her eyes were red from crying.

Peg stood at the threshold. 'I'm sorry for what I said, Veronica.'

'No you're not, Peg. You'll be saying exactly the same again tomorrow.'

'Then I'm sorry it upset you. You're not normally this touchy. Is it that time?' Peg leaned on the door frame.

Veronica rolled her eyes. 'I'm touchy because I'm a widow at the age of thirty-five, with hardly any money, and I have to find a way that Mary and I can survive.'

'You must have known when you married Father that he would probably die a long time before you.'

'I didn't think of that at the time. I . . . I suppose I wanted security. I don't pretend to be the love of your father's life and he probably wasn't the love of mine. He needed a wife to help with his two daughters, and I needed somewhere I could eat regularly.' There was a pair of silk stockings lying on the dressing table. Veronica picked them up and ran them through her fingers. 'It's true I like nice things. I hardly ever had them, you see. I always thought my sister Penelope would take care of me, in the way you and Sheila seem to take care of each other, but that didn't happen.'

'Have you heard from her lately?'

'My niece Cassie writes to me all the time, but Penelope never was much of a letter-writer, especially after her marriage. I thought of suggesting I take Mary to America, but it's been too long since I've seen my sister, and I don't want her to think I'm begging.' She sighed and rested her chin on her palm, looking into the mirror. 'I do wish Uncle Hardwick had thought to share the money between us more evenly. It isn't nice to be the poor relation. But for some reason, he decided that Penelope needed it more.'

'I know that feeling,' said Peg. 'It isn't that I mind Freddie having five hundred pounds a year from Aunt Midchester, but

14

who says that women don't need money just as much as men do? Instead we're expected to get husbands to keep us in our dotage.' Peg crossed the room and patted her stepmother's shoulder, but with her usual lack of finesse she only succeeded in almost knocking Veronica off the footstool. Luckily her stepmother laughed, taking the gesture in the manner intended. 'You know we could go to India,' said Peg. 'They say you can live quite cheaply out there.'

'Peg, we don't get on most of the time. Tomorrow you'll have completely forgotten sympathising with me today. Do you really think we could spend the rest of our lives living in the same house?'

'No, perhaps not.'

'You're not a bad person, Peg. I do realise that. But you and I are never going to be best friends.'

Peg left Veronica perusing her reflection in the mirror and went to her room to finish her letter for her brother, Freddie. She did not tell him about having to sell the house, because she did not want him to feel he had to help them pay the bills.

They had leaned on him more than once in the past, and he had borne it with good grace. But he had more important things to worry about. Instead she told him all the local gossip and about her work on the farm for the war effort. She sealed the letter, got some money for a stamp and made her way to the post office.

Midchester had not changed much since medieval times, regardless of the fact that there were a few motorcars and military vehicles on the streets. The timber-framed houses built during Tudor times still huddled together in a higgledy-piggledy manner. The Quiet Woman pub was even older than the rest, though it too had been modernised and built onto over the years.

'There's been a Yeardley pulling pints in Midchester since Julius Caesar was the emperor of Rome,' the landlord, Frank Yeardley, told customers. There was no documented or archaeological proof of that. Frank just believed it to be so and as he made people happy by selling them ale, no one argued with him.

The newest building was the red brick

village hall next to the church. It had been built when Queen Victoria was alive. The church itself was of Norman origin, but there had been a place of pagan worship on that spot long before then. Unlike Frank at the pub, the church authorities could prove that.

There was a duck pond in the village square and every Monday a cattle market drew visitors from outside of Midchester, especially in summer when the travelling fairs arrived and set up camp on the village green.

Like every small English village, Midchester had its secrets and its sins. The residents, though deferring to the authorities when the need arose, preferred to deal with their own problems. That way they could decide what secrets got out and what remained in the village. It was the only way when everyone was related to everyone else, either by marriage, adultery or incest.

Peg posted her letter and decided to go and look at the old constable's cottage again. Maybe she could manage it alone if she lived frugally and picked up work wherever she could. She was young and strong, so there was plenty of work in her. She went past the pub and saw Frank standing on the doorstep of the Quiet Woman.

'Morning, Miss Bradbourne. If you see our Tom, tell him to get back here, will you? He's supposed to be helping me with a delivery.'

'Will do, Frank.'

'How's young Mister Bradbourne?'

'He was well the last time he wrote. What about your George?' George was Frank's eldest son.

'He was also well the last time I heard from him. But you hear dreadful things, don't you?'

'Yes, yes you do.' Peg felt as if a cloud had gone over the sun. 'We just have to hope it's not as bad as they say.'

'Yep, we do that, miss.'

Peg made her way to Spinsters' Row. Several of the spinsters living in the row were out in their gardens. All had gardeners to do the heavy stuff, but when it came to the care of roses, each considered herself an expert. There was one man living on Spinsters' Row. He was called Colonel Archibald Trent and according to his own estimation had been something big during the Crimean War. A grateful nation had given him a paltry pension that barely allowed him to keep up his subs to his club in London, let alone live the life he had known as a young man.

'Good morning, Miss Bradbourne,' said Miss Cartwright. Miss Cartwright would never admit to being over sixty, but when asked what year she was born, would quite happily tell everyone it was the year Queen Victoria came to the throne, making her almost eighty.

'Good morning, Miss Cartwright.'

'I hear you're thinking of moving here to be alongside us.' The other spinsters had stopped mid-prune to listen to the exchange.

Peg shuddered. Bad news travelled fast. 'Really? From whom?'

'Your sister. She's such a pretty girl. She'll make a fine wife for young Norman Simpson.'

'Yes she will. I had thought of renting

the old constable's cottage. We have to sell the house to pay death duties.'

'Oh yes,' Miss Cartwright twittered. 'Yes indeed, they're awful. Why, I remember when my brother Terence died . . . ' Peg was treated to the story of the terrible fate of Terence's widowed wife and children in the months following his death. Miss Cartwright seemed to delight in the gory details. 'Of course it is terrible when annuities die with you, instead of being given to another member of the family in need, but I don't think that quite excused my sister-in-law up and marrying some other man only six months after poor Terence's death, did it?'

Remembering what her stepmother had said that morning, Peg said charitably, 'Perhaps she did it so that she and the children could eat.'

'Well, yes, I suppose that might be the case, but one must observe the niceties even if it does mean hardship. I'm sure I could have married many times, but I chose virtue over reward. There was that nice young doctor who was here a few years before your dear mother and father returned from India. I was a little older than he, but such things shouldn't matter when one is in love.' Miss Cartwright let out a huge sigh. 'He married a younger woman. They all do in the end. Of course, she had money, which was something I could not offer.' Miss Cartwright sighed at the injustice of it all. 'Still, she was a sweet young thing and devoted to that young daughter of theirs. You know it's an odd thing, but . . . '

Not sure that she wanted to listen to one of Miss Cartwright's tales of failed romance, Peg made a quick getaway.

As she neared the old constable's cottage, Peg comforted herself that it was not quite on Spinsters' Row. It was a little way beyond them, past the station exit and over the railway crossing. There were few homes on that side of the village, and the only one Peg could see from her vantage point was the derelict old house that belonged to Veronica's sister. It was in an even worse condition than the cottage Peg had come to see.

She had reached the gate when she saw Tom Yeardley running hell for leather from that direction. 'Thomas Yeardley, slow down,' she said, holding out her hand and catching his sleeve as he tried to rush past her. He was a well-built boy of seventeen, and showed all the signs of turning into a handsome young man when he was older. 'Your father is looking for you.'

Tom spluttered out the words, pointing in the direction of the other house. 'Miss Bradbourne — a man — dead — up there.'

2

Peg sent Tom back to the village to fetch the new constable, and made her way to the old doctor's house.

'Aren't you afraid, Miss Bradbourne?' Tom had asked her.

'I'm a doctor's daughter, Tom. Death holds no fear for me. Now go on, fetch Constable Archer quickly. You'd better get Doctor Pearson too.'

Peg approached the house, far more nervous than she had let on to Tom. The door, its paint peeling to reveal grey wood beneath, was hanging off the hinges. The aroma of cigarette smoke suggested to Peg what Tom had been doing up there. It was known that many of the young men in the village went there to smoke or drink. Questions had been asked of the local parish council, but as Doctor and Mrs Harrington refused to do anything about the house and ignored all letters asking them for help, there was nothing much the councillors could do.

She pushed open the front door. Held on only by one hinge, it started to fall inwards rather than open. She quickly put it right and went in. She had not thought to ask Tom where the body was, so she had to search every room. Luckily there were only two reception rooms and a kitchen downstairs. There was another door, just behind the drawing room door, but that had been nailed shut. Peg guessed, because the layout in their house was much the same, that the room behind the dining room was where the doctor would see his patients.

She went into what used to be the dining room but it was empty, apart from some old newspapers lying on the floor. Peg guessed that most of those were from tramps that used the house to shelter from the bad weather. She could also see some old cigarette butts and several beer bottles. They might have belonged to the vagrants, but she suspected they were left there by Tom and his friends. Tom would be particularly popular because his father owned a pub. When she stepped into the room, it was not just the smell of cigarettes that assaulted her. The stench of stale urine filled the air. The place had been used as a toilet. She quickly left the room, trying not to gag.

There was another door in the drawing room, which she supposed also led into the surgery area. That too was jammed shut. She noticed that some nails had been put around the outer rim of the door and knocked into the frame, much like the door in the hallway.

There was nothing else in the drawing room apart from some old broken furniture, some of which had been smashed up and burned on the fire. The kitchen was also empty, apart from a few broken plates. If there had been any food in the cupboards, it had long since gone.

The staircase was falling apart, with some of the steps missing, and Peg climbed it carefully so as not to fall through. The higher she climbed, the more nervous she became. She told herself it was ridiculous. She had helped her father deal with his patients and had seen enough death. Yet there was something about coming into this old abandoned house that unnerved her.

She found the body in the smaller front bedroom, lying up against a corner, with blood splattering the wall behind him. In the man's mouth, or what was left of it, was a rifle. He had shot himself. Peg turned her face away for a while until she felt more able to look at him closely.

Instead she took in more of her surroundings. The bedroom was not as badly used by the vagrants as the rest of the house, either because of the rickety stairs or because they preferred to be somewhere they could make a quick getaway if the constable came to move them on.

Some of the wallpaper was still visible. It was pink with blue forget-me-nots, similar to wallpaper her sister Mary had in her room. It had been a child's room then. Why kill himself here? she wondered. Why not downstairs?

She checked behind the door and noticed that there were pencilled lines on the wall. The lower line had writing next to it. The text had faded, but she could just make out the words. They said: '*Cassie, aged 1*'. Someone had charted a child's growth.

There was a pile of fresh vomit near to the window. Tom had looked a bit peaky when she saw him. She wondered how he came to be upstairs. She did not know but she imagined that the boys stayed downstairs, like the tramps. What had brought Tom to this room?

Finally, with her nerves under control, she was able to look at the man more closely. He was definitely not dressed like a tramp. His clothes — a tweed jacket with leather patches on the elbows, and dark trousers — were of good quality. His shoes and socks were missing and she could see scuff marks on the dusty floor where they had been pulled off his feet.

'Someone has been here before,' she murmured. Tom perhaps? He had not been carrying any shoes and socks, but he might have hidden them. But that did not square with his behaviour. The boy really had been horrified, and unsurprisingly given the scene he had come upon.

Peg was just about to search the man's

pocket for proof of identification when Tom returned with the constable. She heard Constable Archer order Tom to wait downstairs.

'He shot himself,' she told him when he made his way up to her.

'Yes, thank you, Miss Bradbourne,' said Constable Archer. 'I can see that. I hope you haven't touched anything.'

'No, I was just about to search him for signs of identification, but I heard you coming.'

'It's a good job I arrived just in time then. You can't mess with evidence, miss.'

'But it's a suicide, not a murder. You can tell the way his hand is clasped around the gun. Father used to do post-mortems for the police. He told me all about it.'

'Good for him. Now if you don't mind, Miss Bradbourne, leave this to me and Doctor Pearson. Take young Tom with you. I'll want to speak to him later. Tell him to wait at the pub for me.'

Reluctantly, Peg left the constable to it. As she was leaving she heard him mutter, 'Every spinster around here thinks she's a detective.'

'Come on, Tom,' she said when she had navigated the dangerous staircase. 'We're not wanted.'

'I don't want to be here anyway,' said Tom as they left the house together. 'It's awful, Miss Bradbourne.' They walked towards the town together.

'What were you doing upstairs, Tom?'

'Nothing, Miss Bradbourne. I mean, just looking around. You know.' Peg suspected that was not the whole story, but she did not want to press him too hard. She doubted very much that Tom Yeardley had shot the man in the bedroom and made it look like suicide. But there was definitely something he was not telling her.

'That old house is dangerous, Tom. You shouldn't have been there at all. Were there any friends with you?'

'No. I haven't got any friends around here.'

'Nonsense. I've seen you with other boys of your age. What about young Percy Fletcher?'

'I hate him,' said Tom. He was close to tears. 'Don't you see? I hate him!' Tom started to run towards town. Peg wanted to catch up with him and ask him why, but she thought better of it. Then she saw Doctor Pearson coming from that direction. She was more interested in talking to him.

Doctor Pearson had to dodge out of the way to avoid Tom crashing into him. 'Morning, Miss Bradbourne. What's got his goat?' he asked in his gentle Scottish brogue. Andrew Pearson had taken over her father's practice about six months earlier. He was an attractive young man in his late twenties and had caused quite a flutter amongst the maidens of Midchester, particularly when they found out that there was not yet a Mrs Pearson.

'Percy Fletcher by all accounts. He hates him.'

'Really? I thought they were best friends.'

'You know what boys are. They have a different best friend every week. It'll be over some girl they both like.' Peg had more important things to consider. 'He shot himself.'

'Who? Tom?' Pearson frowned and

30

looked in the direction Tom had taken.

'No, stupid. The man in the old doctor's house. He put the gun in his mouth and pulled the trigger.'

'Well, I hardly need go and look now, do I?' said Pearson.

'Oh, I suppose you'll have to go and do your stuff. Time of death and all that.'

'You mean you haven't worked all that out?'

'I would have done if Constable Archer hadn't stuck his nose in. But it's an open-and-shut case.'

'Who is he?'

'The man? No idea. He didn't look like anyone from around here. He's well dressed. Apart from the fact his boots and socks are missing. I think some tramp must have taken them.'

'Sounds like it. Well, I'll go and finish off the bits you couldn't manage, shall I?'

'Are you going to say what the constable said about spinsters? Because if you do I might just have to slap you. I couldn't slap him, what with him being a policeman and all that. But you're all right. You're only a doctor.'

'Oh dear. What did the constable say about spinsters?'

'That we all think we're detectives.'

Pearson grinned. 'In a small village like this, the unmarried ladies don't have much else to do.'

'Really?' Peg bristled. 'Of course, because we don't have a husband to dote on, our lives can't possibly have any other meaning, so we're reduced to sticking our noses into other people's business. Is that it?'

'I'm going before I say anything else to upset you.' He tipped his hat. 'Morning, Miss Bradbourne.'

'Damn!' Peg muttered, when he was gone. She stomped one foot on the floor, kicking up the dust on the dirt road. 'Damn, damn, damn.'

When she reached the edge of the village, she could see all the spinsters standing at their gates talking. They looked to her with eyes hungry for information, but she refused to join them. Regardless of what Constable Archer and Doctor Pearson thought, she was not quite ready to join Spinsters' Row yet. The old constable's house could fall down for all she cared. She would find somewhere else to live, with or without a husband.

'Miss Bradbourne,' said Miss Cartwright, 'I really must speak to you. It's about that doctor I mentioned earlier. You see, I wondered — '

'Must hurry,' Peg said abruptly. 'My stepmama is waiting for me.'

She bustled home, furious with herself for caring what Doctor Andrew Pearson thought. Constable Archer's dismissal of her as a spinster detective, though it irked, did not hurt as much. But Constable Archer was a middle-aged man with a chubby round face. Andrew Pearson was young and handsome.

As she neared home, she saw her stepmother getting into an open-topped motorcar. There were so few in Midchester that it was always a talking point when anyone acquired one. Therefore, Peg immediately knew it did not belong to anyone local. A man Peg had never seen before was holding the door open. She could not see his face clearly as he was dressed in the usual driving attire of a flat cap and a scarf wrapped around his face to keep off the flies. Veronica wore a wide-brimmed hat which was held on with a gossamer scarf. Wearing a mauve dress and her favourite lapis lazuli brooch, she looked utterly lovely.

They hardly noticed when they drove past Peg. The man had his eyes on the road, and Veronica was too busy gazing up at him, her eyes full of excitement.

3

'Now, lad, you're not in any trouble,' said Constable Archer. 'Just tell us how you came to find the dead man.'

He was sitting at a table in the dim light of the Quiet Woman pub. In front of him on the table was half a pint of bitter. Tom sat on the bench against the wall, flanked by his father.

'He's already in trouble, Bert,' said Frank. 'He's been warned about going into that house.'

'Boys will be boys,' said Archer sagely. 'I remember the scrapes we used to get into when we were young, Frank. And if he hadn't gone, we wouldn't have known about the man, would we? Then it might have been a little girl or a lady who found him. Ladies are much more sensitive about such things.'

'Miss Bradbourne wasn't from what I hear,' said Frank.

'Miss Bradbourne is a bit different to

35

most ladies. She's a character and that's no mistake. Pity she'll end up an old maid. Men don't much like clever women. Now if you don't mind, Frank, I'd like to talk to Tom alone.' Archer realised it was the only way he would be able to get anything out of the boy, who was clearly inhibited by his father being there. 'I'm sure you've a lot you could be doing.'

'I've a lot he could be helping me with,' said Frank.

'And he will, Frank. Just as soon as me and Tom have had a man-to-man chat.' Frank muttered something unintelligible and went off to the cellar. Constable Archer took his hat off. 'Don't think of me as the local bobby, Tom. Think of me as your Uncle Bert. We're family so you can be honest with me.' Bert was married to Frank's sister, Adeline. 'What were you doing up at the house? Was there anyone else with you?'

'No,' said Tom, a bit too quickly. 'I was on my own.'

'But you lads mostly stay downstairs, don't you? Smoking and drinking beer in the parlour. Don't be afraid to tell me. We know what you all do up there. We don't really care as long as you're not causing trouble in the village. Like I said to our Frank, boys will be boys. So why did you go upstairs this morning?'

'Sometimes we go upstairs. It's like a dare, because they say the house is haunted.'

'I see, lad. So who dared you to go upstairs?'

'No one. I just went up there on my own.'

As far as Bert Archer could tell, Tom was telling the truth, but there was something in the boy's eyes. Some unnamed fear. He decided to leave it alone for a while, aware that the more he pushed, the more Tom would clam up. 'Okay, so you went upstairs. Can you tell me what you found?'

'You know that. It was the dead man.'

'What time might that have been?'

'I don't know. About half past eight, I think.'

'This morning?'

'That's right.'

'You were up late helping your dad last night, weren't you? The pub closed around ten thirty.'

'Yeah. So?'

'And Frank always takes at least an hour to tidy up for the night.'

'That's about right.' Tom looked wary.

'You must have been tired when you went to bed. Then to get up that early in the morning — ?' Archer leaned in. 'So tell me, lad. What time did you creep back out?'

'I didn't . . . ' Tom slumped in his chair, defeated. 'It was about half past midnight. It was a dare, you see. To spend the night in the house on my own.'

'And that's what you did?'

'Yes.'

'Who dared you?'

'I'm not ratting on a . . . a friend.'

'No, no, I get that, lad. You have to stick together. But, er . . . how would they know you'd done the dare if they weren't with you?'

'Someone was supposed to come and see this morning.'

'Someone?'

'Yes, someone. I don't know who. One of the lads.'

'And did they come to the house and check you'd stayed there?'

'I was on my own when I found the dead man.'

It was a question that Archer had not asked, so it immediately made him suspicious. 'Was he wearing his shoes when you found him?'

'I can't remember.' Tom's voice weakened, and whilst he had been mostly evasive with his answers, Archer knew that this was his first real lie.

'Chances are that a man dressed like that would have a nice pair of shoes or boots.' Archer rubbed his chin. 'Don't you think?'

'How would I know?'

'No, no, of course not.'

'Do you think I killed him, Uncle Bert? Is that it?' asked Tom desperately.

'No, lad.' Archer laughed softly. 'Not at all. He killed himself. That's for sure. We just need to find out who he is, that's all. But there was nothing on him. No papers, no pocketbook. It could be that he travelled all the way from wherever-it-was to kill himself. He's not a local. But it's odd that he didn't leave a note.'

'Maybe a tramp stole all his stuff,' said Tom.

'Yes, that's good thinking, lad. A tramp probably stole it all. We'll know more when the doctor can give us a time of death.'

Tom's face turned beetroot-red. 'Can they really say exactly when he died?'

'Well, it's not exact. Not like in the detective novels. But it'll be near enough. So anyway, you found his body and then what?'

'Then I came running down to the village to fetch you and the doctor. I saw Miss Bradbourne on my way.'

'See, that's what's worrying me, Tom. You say you found the man at eight-thirty, but it was after the post office opened at nine that you saw Miss Bradbourne near the old constable's house. I know that, because one of the ladies on Spinsters' Row saw you.'

'I don't know the exact time I found him. I haven't got a watch. I just thought

40

it was about that time.'

'Of course, lad. Well that's all for now. You'll probably have to attend the inquest in a day or two. You go and help your dad.'

Archer watched thoughtfully as Tom lumbered away to help Frank. The boy was hiding something, but whether it had anything to do with the dead man he did not know. It might have just been something illegal he and his friends had been up to. All Archer could do was keep a lookout.

* * *

Tom went out into the yard behind the pub and took a long, deep breath. He was about to go back inside when he saw a plume of smoke coming from behind the wall at the end of the yard. The gate was open. Percy Fletcher stuck his head around the gap. 'Come here,' he said.

Tom reluctantly went to him, hating himself even as he gave in to the other boy's malevolence. Percy was not even as tall as Tom, but he was twice as wide and three times more threatening.

'What you said?' Percy caught Tom by his collar the moment he drew nearer. At the same time, Fletcher looked around to make sure no one was looking.'

'Nothing. I've told them nowt.'

'Good. I'm onto a nice little earner here, and you had better not ruin it for me.'

'I've told them nowt,' Tom repeated, his throat constricting.

'If I find out you've talked . . . ' Percy drew his fist back and punched Tom full in the stomach, before sauntering off up the alleyway behind the pub.

Winded, Tom fell to a crouch, with tears streaming from his eyes.

★   ★   ★

Archer strolled back to the police station, via Spinsters' Row. He kept his head up, facing forward, determined not to catch the eye of any of the old biddies standing in their gardens.

He was relieved to pass Colonel Trent and see that the good fellow had his head down, gardening.

'Good morning, Colonel,' he said as he passed by. The colonel looked up and nodded curtly. 'Nice day,' Archer offered.

Some sound emitted from the colonel's throat, which could either have been a yes or a no. Archer was not sure.

'Oh, Constable Archer,' said Miss Cartwright, opening her gate and stepping out into the lane. 'I really need to speak to you.'

'I'm in rather a hurry,' said Archer.

'But it is important, you see. About the dead man.'

To the left of Archer, the Colonel muttered something about nosy women and threw his rake down, retreating to his house. He stopped by his front door to take off his muddy boots. Archer noticed that they had holes in the bottom. Poor old soul, thought Archer. A man of the colonel's courage reduced to such penury was a sad sight to see.

'What about the dead man, Miss Cartwright?'

'I did try to tell Miss Bradbourne this morning. That girl is always in such a hurry to go nowhere. Not like her sister, Miss Sheila Bradbourne. She is a real lady. Poor Miss Bradbourne will never marry, of course, but her sister will do well with young Norman.'

'What has Miss Bradbourne's spinster status to do with the dead man?' asked Archer.

'Why, nothing. Though my own status has much to do with him.'

'Did you kill him, Miss Cartwright?'

'Oh the very thought,' she twittered. 'Of course not — even if he did pass me over for a younger lady with money. Of course, when a man is twenty . . . ten . . . years older than a woman, no one minds, but if a woman is older than a man, people talk. I did not mind, but he did. Strange though. I did not expect him to return to Midchester.'

'Who, Miss Cartwright?'

'I saw him pass my house yesterday and as soon as I heard about the dead man up at his old house, I knew it was him.'

'Who?'

'Surely you must remember him. It was Doctor Arthur Harrington.'

4

Peg sliced the spade through the earth, working out all her anger and frustration on the fields alongside Bedlington Hall. With Sheila working at the school, and Mary in her own class, there was no one she could talk to about Veronica and the strange man.

She wanted to know who he was and what his appearance meant. Mostly she was angry that Veronica had not even waited a year after William Bradbourne's death before finding someone else. It was all very well understanding about Miss Cartwright's sister-in-law finding a new husband, but this was different. This was her father and she would not have his memory slighted in such a way. The man was probably rich, and that was why Veronica had latched onto him. Peg put no store by the admiring looks her stepmother gave the man. She had looked at Peg's father that way, and yet only a few months after his death, she was with another man.

'Got a letter for you, Miss Bradbourne,' said a voice from the gate leading into the field. Peg straightened up and saw the postman, Abe Potter. 'From your brother, I reckon. I was on my way down the house but I reckoned you might want to read it in your break.'

'Thank you, Abe,' said Peg, going to the gate. 'I need cheering up.'

'I hope it's good news then,' said Abe.

'Why? Is there any reason it shouldn't be?' Peg held out her hand for the letter. A cloud seemed to roll over the sun. 'It is a letter, is it not? Not a telegram?'

'Ay, it's a letter. Not that a few telegrams haven't gone out this morning.'

'Really? Who to?'

'The Simpsons. Their lad Barney has copped it. Only their Len is left now and he'll be old enough to go soon. And the Fletchers. Their son Teddy died. They've only got Percy left. I'm glad my Herbie is not old enough to go, and that our Maggie is a girl and still in her cradle. Otherwise we'd have no children left in Midchester at all.'

'Thanks, Abe. You're a real Job's comforter, do you know that?' Peg snatched the letter from him.

'Now, Miss Bradbourne, don't take on so. You did ask me.'

'Yes, I suppose I did. Remind me not to ask you next time.' Peg smiled sadly. She patted him on the shoulder in her usual abrupt way. 'It'll all be over before Herbie is old enough, I'm sure of it. And I can't imagine them ever letting women fight on the front line. I wish they would. I'd give the Kaiser what-for.'

'I bet you would, Miss. Good morning to you.'

'Morning, Abe.'

Peg put the letter in her pocket until lunchtime. When noon came, she sat down on a fallen tree stump and first opened up her jam sandwich and a bottle of stout. Then as she munched her sandwich, she read the letter from her brother, Freddie.

Dear Peggy-Lou,
I hope you're well, dearest. It's pretty much hell here, as always, but as I can't tell you where here is, I won't bore you

with the details. We've lost quite a few of the lads, some from Midchester, but you probably know that by now. It's that chaotic here, you probably find out their identities before I do.

What you probably won't know yet is that Teddy Fletcher deserted. When they found him, I tried to speak up for him. Said the lad was afraid, like we all were. It's bloody awful here. But they shot him anyway. Rum job, really. Has to be done, otherwise discipline would fall apart. But, still. Not good. We're not allowed to say it out loud. Queen and country and all that, you know. Feel like taking off myself sometimes, but I decided that if I was going to get shot I might as well take out a few of the hun while I was at it.

Anyway, enough of the misery here. How are you? Sheila told me that Veronica wants to sell the house to pay off some debts. If you can persuade her to wait till I get home on leave, we might be able to sort something out. Can't do much from here really. You know how it is. But anyway, don't worry, *Pet*. If anything happens to me, I've made sure you, *Sheila* and *Mary* will be alright. Not rich, but I've put enough by for you just in case. My friends say I might marry, but that's only because they don't know me like you do. I thought about it. Find a nice girl and settle down. But I'd be lying to her and myself, wouldn't I? Odd how I can say things to you that I can't say to *Sheila*.

You haven't told her that other stuff have you? No, of course you haven't. Sorry, *Pet*. A man gets to thinking things here. About what people might find out about him when he's dead. And if people knew the truth, well it wouldn't matter how heroic I was, would it? They'd just know that one thing about me and forget all the rest. Not that I plan any heroics. I'm just hanging on and hoping not to get shot, just like every other poor bugger here.

I seem to have got a bit morose, old girl. What else did I have to tell you? Oh yes, Lieutenant *Gerald Sanderson*. He's from *Devon*. Or is it *Dorset?* I forget now. One of the D's down south where we've got extended family. He was injured last week — poor bloke shot in the leg — and he's on his way to Bedlington Hall to stay at the military hospital. He owns the place, so that's a bit of a coincidence. It was entailed to him when Great Aunt Bedlington died. He's the son of her stepdaughter. You know, the one with the insane husband. I'm not sure if that makes him related to us or not (being the son of Great Aunt's stepdaughter, not his old pa being insane, ha ha!). But he is sort of related so I told him you'd look in on him. He's a nice chap. So go and say hello if you can.

I have to go now, Peggy-Lou. I miss talking to you properly, but one day I'll get some leave and we can talk away to our heart's content, just like we used to.

Your loving brother
Freddie

Peg read the letter through several times, as she always did when Freddie's letters arrived. He seldom said anything about the situation where he was, so she spent a lot of time reading between the lines. His forced cheerfulness was not lost on her, and neither were his fears about what people might find out about him when he died.

She kissed the letter. 'They'll never hear it from me, dearest.'

Able to come and go from the farm as she pleased, Peg decided to take the afternoon off and walk over to Bedlington Hall to meet Gerald Sanderson. If Freddie liked him, she was sure to. It was at the back of her mind that he might be able to help them with their problem. Not that she intended to go cap-in-hand. Great Aunt Bedlington had always helped her mother and father, sending game and other consumables to the house, and inviting them to dinner several nights a week. It went a long way to helping with the housekeeping of a country doctor and his wife. If Gerald Sanderson only allowed her to have the odd partridge and some vegetables from the hall gardens, it would cut down on her food bill.

Although the farm was alongside Bedlington Hall, it was by no means a simple trek through the fields. High hedges barred the direct route. Peg suspected it was because some Lord Midchester in the past did not want to have to watch the serfs make his money for him. She was forced to walk via the narrow country lanes, back through Midchester and up to the house's main entrance from behind the churchyard and village hall. The house had been turned into a military hospital only a few months before. Because it was a reasonable day, some of the men sat outside. They were flanked by pretty nurses and cheerful orderlies.

When she reached the main door, Doctor Pearson was just coming out to his car. 'We must stop meeting this way,' he said.

'Have you been doing your rounds?' asked Peg, before mentally kicking herself. Of course he had. Why else would he be up at the military hospital?

'Yes, I have. What brings you here?'

'I'm looking for my cousin, Gerald Sanderson.'

'Ah, yes, I've just seen him. I didn't realise you were related. He's not taking visitors at the moment.'

'Why not? Is he very badly hurt?' Peg had seen some of the soldiers who had been in explosions.

'Not physically — a bit of shrapnel here and there and a bullet to the shoulder — but psychologically he's a mess, like many of the young men. He's had a tough time of it. He was on his way home with one injury and then their transport crashed, killing everyone else. He's the only one who made it.'

'How awful,' said Peg, instantly feeling guilty about wanting to sponge off a man who had been through so much. 'Perhaps I'd better go away and come back another day. What happened about the man Tom found this morning? Was it definitely suicide?'

'As far as I can tell. I'll be doing the post-mortem later, but I was needed here first. Why? Do you suspect something else?'

'I don't know. Tom acted strange, that's all. I don't think he killed the man, but I think he knew more than he let on.'

'Yes, Constable Archer thinks the same. These youngsters always get an idea that if they say something, the world will collapse. Generally it turns out to be nothing at all. Anyway, I'd best get on.'

'Yes, I suppose I should too.' Peg glanced up at the Hall just in time to see a man standing in one of the upper windows, looking in her direction. He was very handsome, with fair hair and blue eyes. He smiled at Peg and it was as if the sun became a little brighter.

She forgot about Doctor Pearson until he spoke again. 'Well, it looks like you've found your cousin. That's the first time I've seen him smile since he got here.'

'That's him?' Peg changed her mind about going home, and went into the hall without bothering to say goodbye to Pearson. She would meet Gerald Sanderson and she would be the one to cheer him up. She owed it to Freddie.

'Yes, I realise he doesn't want to see anyone,' Peg was saying to the strict nurse who met her in the main entrance, 'but we're related. I mean, he doesn't actually know me. We've never met, but . . . '

'It's okay, nurse,' said a friendly voice behind her. 'I'll see her. After all, I can't turn family away.'

Peg turned to face Gerald Sanderson. 'Hello,' she said, feeling her heart flutter a little.

'Hello. I'm sorry, but . . . '

'Oh, of course. Silly me. I'm Freddie's sister, Peg. Well it's Margaret Louise actually, but no one calls me that.'

'Freddie Bradbourne, right?' He frowned.

'Yes, that's right.'

'Well it's nice to meet you, Miss Bradbourne.'

'There's no need to stand on ceremony. Call me Peg. We are related, after all. Can I call you Gerald?'

'I prefer Gerry.'

'Gerry it is, then. It is good to meet you.' He held a walking stick with one hand, so Peg took his other hand and pumped it up and down before noticing him wince and rub his shoulder.

'Sorry,' he said. 'Got a bit of shrapnel in the shoulder.'

'Oh, of course. Sorry. Shall we go and

sit outside and talk? You must tell me all about where you and Freddie have been. He won't say anything in his letters, you see, and I worry so much about him.'

'You'd worry more if I told you what things are like out there,' said Gerry.

'Oh but you see, I won't. It's the not knowing that's the worst bit. Once I know I can deal with it.'

Half an hour later they sat in the grounds of Bedlington Hall drinking tea provided by one of the young nurses. 'It didn't take you long to wrap her around your little finger,' said Peg when the nurse had gone.

'They're all very kind to me. So, tell me more about this suicide and the mystery of the missing boots.'

'You're not like other men.'

'I'm not?'

'No, most young men like to just talk about themselves. Yet all you've done is ask me questions about my life. In the last half hour you've found out about my two sisters, that I don't get on with my stepmother — except for the rare times when I do — and that I'm thinking of living in the worst house in the village. I know very little about you.'

'The truth is, Peg, I don't remember much about me. Oh, I know my name and that I'm from Devon and that both my parents are dead, which leaves me heir to Bedlington Hall. But everything else is blurry.'

'Do you remember if you have a sweetheart or not?'

'I'm pretty certain I don't. But I couldn't swear to it and I wouldn't like to mislead anyone on that point.' There was a gentle warning in his voice and a little sadness behind his eyes. 'So, tell me,' he said, becoming more jocular. 'Who do you think is wearing the dead man's boots?'

5

'I think he finds the truth too painful,' Peg said. She was sitting on the edge of Sheila's bed whilst Sheila sat at the dressing table, going through her night-time beauty routine. 'That's why he kept deflecting it. I think they call it survivor's guilt. When someone is the only one to live after a catastrophe. You really must meet him, Sheila. He's wonderful and so charming.'

Sheila rubbed cream into her face and hands. 'Maybe we could persuade Veronica to invite him for dinner one night when he's feeling better.'

'Oh her. I'd almost forgotten.'

'Forgotten what?'

'She was getting into a man's car this morning. And worse still, she seemed to like it.'

'Really?' Sheila spun around on the chintz stool, her eyes bright. 'Who was it?'

'You don't look as horrified as you should, Sheila.'

'Why should I be horrified? Veronica is still a young woman.'

'A woman who has only been a widow for six months.'

'Oh, Peg.' Sheila sighed. 'What did you expect? She wasn't the love of Papa's life and he wasn't the love of hers. They married out of convenience: Papa because he had us to look after, and her because she was one of the genteel poor, from a class which frowns upon women working. You saw the raised eyebrows when I decided to become a teacher. They were raised even higher when you went to work up at the farm. At least we are young enough to make our own way in this new world if we have to. At her age, and with no skills, all Veronica can do to survive is to marry again.'

'I can't believe you're not disgusted with her.' Peg pouted. 'It's disgraceful behaviour, that's what it is. We don't even know who he is or if he'll be a good father to Mary.'

'Dearest, you are rather putting the cart before the horse. You saw her with a man once.'

'She's in love with him. Or at least she's acting as if she is, which is bad enough.'

'Well good for Veronica, that's all I can say. Don't you want anyone to be happy, Peg?'

'Of course I do.'

'No, I don't think you do. You want us to all stay with you and for nothing to change, even if it means me not marrying Norman and Veronica not marrying whoever this man is that she's seeing. But what does it matter if we're poor and unhappy all our lives? As long as Peg Bradbourne doesn't have to live alone.'

'That's a very cruel thing to say, Sheila.'

'The truth usually is, dearest.'

Peg jumped up off the bed. 'Well, I shall just go — alone — to my room, where I shall read — alone — and think of how happy I am going to be when I move into my new home — wherever that may be — alone.'

'Don't hate me for being honest with you, Peg.' Sheila held out her hand. 'You know I love you dearly. I just don't see the world in the same black-and-white terms as you do. You just want Midchester and everyone in it to remain the same, forever, and that can't happen. Especially with this war. It's changing us all and when it's over we shall never be the same again.'

Peg took Sheila's hand in both of hers and kissed it. 'I'll never hate you, darling, no matter what you say to me. You, Freddie and Mary are the only people I truly love.' She let go, reluctantly, and went to the door. 'I do think we need to know who this man is.'

'Then ask Veronica about him. Just do it tactfully.'

'I can be tactful.'

'No you cannot. But please try not to make her feel like the whore of Babylon when you do ask.'

Peg poked out her tongue and went out onto the gas-lit landing. It was very dim as they had not put electricity in the house, but she could see candlelight shining under Veronica's door. As she approached her stepmother's room the light went out. It stopped Peg in her tracks. Veronica was not yet asleep, as she had only just put the light out, but it seemed wrong somehow to go and disturb her. Not really fancying an argument just before bed, Peg decided to wait until daylight.

★ ★ ★

Veronica did a good job of keeping out of Peg's way for the next few days, as if realising her stepdaughter wanted words with her. By the time Peg came down to breakfast on Saturday morning, Veronica had gone. Sheila and Mary had nearly finished their food.

'Where is Veronica?'

'Mary said she went out early,' said Sheila.

'Where to, Mary?'

'I don't know, Peg. A telegram came for her and then she rushed out, very happy.'

'She'll have gone to see that man!' Peg dropped heavily into a seat at the dining table. 'At this time of the morning too. It's preposterous.'

'What man?' asked Mary.

'It seems Mama has a suitor,' Sheila said gently, firing a warning glance at Peg.

'Oh how romantic,' said Mary. 'Who is he?'

'We don't know,' said Peg. 'Has Mama said anything to you about it?'

Mary shook her head. 'No, but when she kissed me farewell, she said that we didn't have to worry anymore and that everything would be all right.'

'So she is going to marry him.' Peg sighed. 'Well he'd better be a good father to you, Mary, or he'll have me to answer to.'

'It will be nice to have a papa again,' Mary said. 'I didn't have very long with ours. Not like you and Sheila.'

Peg reached over and took Mary's hand. 'I know, darling.' She had been so selfish, thinking of her own feelings, that she had failed to consider Mary's. The child was very loving, and needed a father who would love her too. Peg only hoped that Veronica's paramour was happy and willing to take on a young daughter.

Veronica did not return that day, or that evening.

'I don't understand it,' Peg said to Sheila on the Sunday morning as they helped Izzy the maid prepare breakfast in the kitchen. She waited a moment until Izzy had left the room. 'Do you think we should call Constable Archer?'

'What shall we say? If she has spent the night with this man, she would not thank us for drawing attention to it. Think of the shame.'

'The shame would be hers, not ours,' said Peg truculently.

'Even so, Peg, we cannot subject her to that. We must do something, and Constable Archer is discreet.'

Peg picked up the tray of tea things. 'Whatever I may think of Veronica — and lord knows we have had our differences — I cannot believe she would do this to Mary. The poor child was distraught last night.'

'I'm going to phone the constable,' said Sheila. 'Whether you like it or not.'

Half an hour later, Constable Archer arrived. They took him to the drawing room. 'We're sorry to bother you on a Sunday morning,' said Sheila. 'It is a very delicate matter.' She coughed and blushed. 'I hardly know where to start . . . '

'Veronica has gone out all night with a strange man and not returned,' Peg blurted out.

'We do not know that she is with a man,' Sheila said, her eyes flashing angrily at Peg. 'But we do hope we can rely on your discretion if that turns out to be the case, Constable Archer.'

'Of course,' said Archer, bowing his head courteously. 'Who is the man you think Mrs Bradbourne went to meet?'

'We don't know,' said Peg. 'I saw him pick her up the other day, but he was muffled up so I didn't see his face. He drove a bullnose Morris Cowley in green, fourteen hundred and ninety-five cc, with a four-cylinder engine.'

Archer raised his eyebrows.

'What? You think that because I'm a woman I don't know motorcars?'

'Not at all, Miss Bradbourne. I am often surprised by the things you know. There cannot be many men in the area who drive motorcars.'

'He'd also be very old, I should think,'

said Peg. 'Otherwise he would be away fighting the war, wouldn't he?'

It was Archer's turn to cough delicately. 'Some of us would like to, Miss.'

'Oh, of course.' Peg nodded. 'I'm not suggesting otherwise. I'm just making a point that most of our men are off fighting the war, so there can't be many other eligible men of Veronica's age or older in the area. Of course he could be young and have medical reasons, I suppose. But it's a start.'

'And you say she received a telegram yesterday morning. If we could find out the details of that, it might be a start. I'll check with the telegram operator. May I use your telephone?'

A few minutes later, Archer came from the hallway, looking perplexed. 'I've had a word with Miss Watson at the exchange and she says that no telegram was sent to this house yesterday morning.'

'But Izzy, our maid, said that Veronica had received a telegram,' said Sheila. 'I'll call her.'

'It was a telegram, Mr Archer,' said Izzy, when they had questioned her. 'A

66

man brought it to the house.'

'Who?'

'I don't know, sir,' Izzy said. 'He wasn't local, but I supposed that Miss Watson had got in some help, what with there being so many telegrams lately.'

'What did he look like?'

'I don't know, sir.'

'So not young and good-looking,' said Peg, with a grin, knowing Izzy's propensity to fall for every handsome errand boy in Midchester.

'I can't say, Miss Bradbourne. He was wearing a scarf around his face. I thought it was odd, with it being so warm of late.'

'So someone who didn't want to be recognised,' said Archer.

'The scarf around the face suggests it's the man Veronica met the other day,' said Peg. 'He probably hid his car around the corner somewhere.'

'If it is him . . . ' Archer paused, looking at Izzy.

'That will be all, Izzy, thank you,' said Peg.

'If it is him, then it may be that Mrs Bradbourne has decided to stay with him,' said Archer. 'I would advise against sending out a search party yet, ladies, in case it does cause embarrassment.'

'Thank you, Constable Archer,' said Sheila. 'You are very kind.'

Veronica did not return that night or the night after.

'I fear it's time for the search party,' said Sheila on the Tuesday morning.

Peg nodded sadly. 'Yes, I think so too. Whatever I may think of Veronica, she would never have abandoned Mary like this. I'll ring the constable . . . '

She had just reached the telephone in the hall when there was a knock on the front door. She opened it to find Constable Archer standing there with several of his officers. 'Miss Bradbourne . . . Peg . . . ' he said gently, having known her since she was a little girl. 'We have found Mrs Bradbourne. I'm sorry . . . '

6

It rained on the day of Veronica's funeral. The family — Peg, Sheila and Mary — led the mourners into the church. There were no other relatives, only townspeople who had known the Bradbourne family for years. Peg had written to America to let Penelope Harrington know her sister was dead, but had received no reply.

'The poor woman is probably still reeling about losing her husband in such dreadful circumstances,' Sheila had said the night before, when she visited Peg's bedroom. 'Now her sister committing suicide too.' Sheila had shuddered and jumped into the double bed beside her sister. It was something they used to do as children, and showed how vulnerable Sheila was feeling. 'Poor Mary. She's barely spoken since it happened. What if Mrs Harrington wants to take her, Peg?'

'We shan't let her.'

'She's her aunt and probably her legal guardian. I'm not sure how it works.'

'We shan't let her,' Peg insisted.

Due to the nature of Veronica's death it had taken a lot of pressure to persuade the Church to let her be buried, but her standing in the community, as the widow of a well-loved doctor, was such that the Bishop had given special dispensation due to the results of the inquest.

The inquest found that Veronica had taken an overdose of laudanum, but as no one could confirm that the lady had been in a suicidal state, they declared an open verdict. Peg suspected this was as much to spare the family as any real doubts.

'It's a rum do,' Peg heard Frank Yeardley say. After the interment he walked over to Peg and Sheila. 'I know you've had a lot on, with the police sniffing around the house, so I've laid on some sandwiches and sherry at the pub.'

'That's very kind, Mr Yeardley,' said Sheila. 'You must let us know how much we owe you.'

'Nowt, lass . . . I mean Miss Bradbourne. You don't owe me owt.' 'Thank you, Frank,' said Peg, with a wan smile.

'If there's anything else I can do, you just let me know. You girls don't have to go short of anything.'

Except our home, thought Peg, but did not say so. Veronica had left very little, and Peg and Sheila's combined income would not be enough for the upkeep of a six-bedroom family house. They had even had to let Izzy go.

'You're a good man,' Peg said. 'Come on, Mary, darling. I'll get you some pop, shall I?'

When she tried to take Mary's hand, the child snatched it away from her. 'I don't want to go with you!' she cried. 'You never liked mummy anyway.'

Mary stormed off down the path, closely followed by Sheila. All Peg could do was watch, with her heart breaking in two. She felt a comforting hand on her shoulder.

'She's had a shock, Peg,' said Gerald Sanderson. 'She'll come around.'

'She hates me,' Peg moaned.

'No, she doesn't. Come on, let's go the pub. You need a drink, and so do I.'

71

'It was good of you to come, Gerry. It's not as if you knew Veronica.'

'She was family.'

'Well, not really.'

'By marriage then. And even if she wasn't, you are.' He held out his arm and Peg took it as they walked out of the churchyard and towards the centre of the town where the pub was situated. 'Any news on the man Veronica went off with?'

'No, nothing. Oh, Gerry, it was so awful, how they found her. She was in a sleazy little hotel — the type that illicit lovers use — and she had taken an overdose of laudanum. He must have ended the relationship and left her bereft. Oh, if I ever find that man!'

'But you did hate her?'

Peg pulled her hand away from his arm. 'I didn't wish her dead!'

'No, of course not. Sorry, Peg.' Gerry took her arm again and made a point of putting it back in his. It felt nice walking next to him, as if they were a couple.

'And I didn't really hate her. I just resented her for coming into our lives and trying to take Mother's place. She was a silly woman in many ways, with her spending habits and wish for pretty things, but I don't think there was any real harm in her. It's all very odd, isn't it?'

'What is?'

'First of all her brother-in-law, Arthur Harrington, returns to Midchester and takes his own life, and then she commits suicide too.'

'You think there's some connection?'

'I don't know, but it's a bit of a coincidence, isn't it?'

'Maybe he was her illicit lover and when he died, she wanted to die too.'

'Don't be ridiculous. I saw her with the man after Harrington was found dead. Besides, Harrington had been in America for twenty years or more.'

Frank Yeardley was as good as his word. In the pub a table was laid out with sandwiches and fruit cake, and everyone was given a small glass of sherry as they entered.

'Thank you, Tom,' said Peg, taking a drink from the boy.

'I'm very sorry for your loss, Miss

73

Bradbourne,' said Tom.

'Thank you.'

'Peg . . . ' Doctor Pearson extricated himself from two of the spinsters and came over to her. 'I want to tell you how very sorry I am.'

'Thank you, Doctor Pearson. You remember Mr Sanderson, my cousin, of course.'

'Good to see you up and about, Mr Sanderson.' Pearson and Gerry shook hands.

'I wanted to support Peg today, her being family and all that.'

'I'd like to have a chat with you about Bedlington Hall, if I may. I have plans for the continuation of hospital, and clearly you're now the man to ask.'

'Not today,' said Gerry curtly.

Pearson seemed taken aback. 'I didn't mean to be indelicate.' He looked at Peg, his handsome face reddening.

'We know,' Peg said with a tight smile. 'Anyway, I might be asking Gerry for a place to stay soon, so get in the queue.' She, too, coloured up when she realised what she had said and what it might imply to Gerry. 'I mean lodgings.'

All lost for words, they stood silently drinking their sherry. Pearson looked as if he was just about to speak when he stopped, looking towards the doorway.

It seemed that the sun had come out, and not only that, but had brought with it a young woman of such outstanding beauty that all the men assembled could do nothing but gape. She had strawberry-blonde hair, with large green eyes framed by dark lashes. She was dressed more for a wedding than a funeral, in a white muslin dress with a wide-brimmed blue hat and gloves. A silk sash around the dress matched the hat and gloves.

'Oh, excuse me,' she said with an American accent. 'I'm looking for the local constable. I was told I might find him here.'

'Please, do come in,' said Pearson as he rushed to help her. Several other men did the same, including Gerry Sanderson. Peg tutted and sighed. 'May I get you a chair to sit on?'

'Are you the constable?' the girl asked, looking up at Pearson with obvious admiration.

'No, I'm Doctor Pearson. Constable Archer is around somewhere . . . And you are?'

'I'm here about my father but I seem to have interrupted . . . ' She looked around. 'Oh, I'm so sorry. Is this a wake?'

'Yes, it is,' said Peg, stepping forward, deftly pushing men out of the way as she did so. 'Who is your father?'

'Doctor Arthur Harrington. We had word he was found dead . . . ' The girl's green eyes filled up with tears. It had a charming effect, and a wave of men moved towards her again. Peg harrumphed. The girl was a regular damsel in distress.

'Cassandra?' said Peg, frowning. 'You're Cassandra Harrington?'

'Yes, but please call me Cassie. And you are?'

'I'm Peg Bradbourne. Your cousin . . . sort of. Over there is my sister, Sheila and our little sister, Mary.' The awful truth suddenly hit Peg. 'Cassie, has no one told you? I did send a message but . . . '

'What is it? What's happened to Aunt Veronica?'

'She died a few days ago.' Peg hesitated

76

to give the cause of death.

'Oh my,' said Cassie. 'How awful . . . Can I . . . Please Doctor Pearson, I'd rather like that chair now.'

Pearson led her to a chair. Several people sitting at the table vacated it so that Peg, Sheila and Andrew could sit with Cassie. Everyone made a big show of going about the business of eating and drinking, but it was clear that the villagers were fascinated by the goddess who had walked into the Quiet Woman pub. Mary had also come out of herself a little and stood nearby, watching Cassie avidly.

'Have a glass of sherry,' said Pearson. 'It will do you good.'

'Thank you. Poor Mary, you darling,' said Cassie, holding out her arms. Mary ran into them, accepting Cassie as if she had known her all her life.

Peg folded her arms and harrumphed. Sheila kicked her under the table. 'I wrote to America,' Peg explained.

'But we're not in America.'

'I can see that,' said Peg.

'What I mean is, we've been in England for several months. My father wanted to come over and visit the old country. He left us in Liverpool to come here, saying that he wanted to come ahead and prepare for us to return. I never dreamed he would do such a thing. And now Aunt Veronica. She wrote to me all the time, telling me about England. I was so looking forward to meeting her.'

'You say us,' said Sheila. 'You and . . . ?'

'Mother. She's still in Liverpool. I travelled down by train this morning, wanting to make some sense of what happened to Father before she arrived. And now this . . . '

'You've had a dreadful shock,' said Pearson. 'Drink your sherry.'

'Yes, do,' said Gerry. 'It will make you feel better.'

'I'm sure she's quite capable of deciding when she wants to drink,' said Peg.

'Peg . . . ' Sheila's voice had the gentle warning tone it took on every time Peg was in danger of going too far. 'Where are you staying, Cassie?'

'I thought to book into a hotel, if there is one.'

'Not in Midchester, but some of the ladies on Spinsters' Row do let rooms,' said Peg, believing she was being helpful.

'We have six bedrooms,' Sheila said pointedly. 'Cassie is family, Peg.'

Not ours, thought Peg, disgusted by the way Doctor Pearson and Gerry Sanderson were fawning over her. 'Okay,' she said, giving one of her tight smiles. 'She can stay with us.'

'I wouldn't want to intrude.'

You already have, thought Peg, looking miserably at Andrew Pearson and Gerry Sanderson. It was bad enough having a prettier sister. Adding a stunning American belle to the mix left Peg with no chance with the two best-looking men in Midchester.

She stood up and went outside, needing to get away on her own for a while. She found herself wandering along Spinsters' Row, looking at the old constable's cottage again. Maybe it was where she belonged. Men had never fawned over her the way they did over Sheila and Cassie. Mary also showed signs of growing up to be a beauty. She heard her father's voice asking her gently, 'Do you want them to fawn over you, Peg?'

'Just a little bit would be nice,' she murmured to herself. 'Just sometimes.'

As she ambled slowly along the row, she saw Tom Yeardley and Percy Fletcher in the distance. They seemed to be having an argument, but when Percy saw Peg, he put his arm around Tom's shoulder as if they were suddenly the best of friends again. Only Tom's face belied that.

'Is everything all right, boys?' she asked, her eyes narrowing.

'Everything's fine, Miss Bradbourne,' said Percy. 'I'm really sorry for your loss.'

'Thank you.' Something about the boy made Peg bristle. There was malevolence in his eyes. 'Tom, could I have a word, please? In private?'

'I know when I'm not wanted,' Percy said, affecting a jocular tone. Peg could see that in reality he was livid. There was something else in his eyes. Was it fear?

She and Tom waited until he was well out of earshot. It took some time, as Percy seemed to walk slowly, as if trying to listen to what Peg had to say. He might have taken even longer, but away in the distance Cassie Harrington stepped out of the Quiet Woman. Even a sullen boy like Percy was not immune to such beauty, so his step quickened so that he could, presumably, get a closer look at her.

'Is Percy bothering you, Tom?' asked Peg.

'No, Miss Bradbourne.'

'I think he is. If you ever need to talk about it, you can trust me, you know.'

'Thank you, Miss Bradbourne, but there's nothing wrong.' Tom's voice trembled as he spoke.

'Very well. If you don't want to tell me, I can't force you. But you know that bullies are best confronted, Tom, and I know that Percy Fletcher is a bully, no matter how many times he doffs his cap at me.'

'I'd best get back and help my dad. He doesn't know I've come out.'

Peg watched him as he walked back to the pub, with his shoulders slumped in defeat. Something was amiss, but she could not put her finger on it.

She had a feeling, because so much seemed to be connected in the past week or so, that it had something to do with finding Arthur Harrington. Had Percy been there? And if so, what did Percy not want people to know? And whilst Percy might be a bully, he was not a murderer. The coroner had confirmed that Harrington's death was by suicide.

Percy might not be a murderer, but he had been known to be light-fingered.

Peg started her own walk back to town, passing by Colonel Trent's garden as she did. The old man was digging a flower bed. As he lifted his foot to place it on the spade, she noticed he was wearing a new pair of boots.

7

'Tell us all about yourself,' said Sheila, handing Cassie a cup of coffee. 'What do you remember of Midchester?' Mary had gone to bed soon after dinner, leaving the three older girls to talk in private in the drawing room.

'Not much at all,' said Cassie. 'We left when I was about four years old, I think. America is my home now. Father had a practice in New York. He mostly dealt with neurotic rich women, but he said it paid better than some crummy hospital in the sticks.'

'What brought you back to Britain?' asked Peg.

'Father wanted to show me home.'

'Odd time, during a war,' said Peg. 'Weren't you afraid of your boat being sunk by the Germans? Especially after what happened to the *Lusitania*.'

'Father was adamant we come, and one did not argue with him.' For the first time, Cassie's bright eyes became dark. Then she brightened again. 'The captain took the necessary precautions.'

'Was your father the sort of man who would take his own life?' asked Peg.

'I'm afraid I don't know,' Cassie replied. 'You see ... the thing is ... Father and Mother lived mostly separate lives. He had his practice and Mother had her own interests. I was sent to boarding school at the age of six, and spent most of the vacations with my friends' families. I'm afraid my father was something of a mystery to me.'

'Will your mother be coming to Midchester?' asked Sheila. 'Now that your aunt is dead?'

'She said she will come for Father's funeral. She doesn't yet know about my aunt. I suppose I should telephone and let her know, but I can hardly bring myself to break the news. They weren't especially close, but Aunt Veronica was Mother's sister.'

'Do you have a beau?' asked Sheila. Peg tutted to herself.

'No, I don't have a beau. There was

someone, but ... well he married someone else.'

'You were jilted?' asked Peg.

'Peg!' Not for the first time, Sheila surreptitiously kicked her sister in the shins.

'No, I broke it off. I wasn't ready to marry. I think I wanted to come to England and find out who I am before giving up my name altogether. Does that sound silly to you?'

'No, it doesn't,' said Peg thoughtfully. It seemed that Cassie Harrington was not the silly airhead that Peg first believed her to be. 'Too many woman rush into marriage ... ' She gave her sister a meaningful look. 'And don't find out what they want to be.'

'Being a wife and mother is important,' said Sheila. 'The most important roles a woman can play.'

'Someone should have told my mother that,' said Cassie darkly.

'What do you mean?' asked Peg. She remembered the upstairs room in the Harringtons' old house, with Cassie's height recorded on the wall. She began to wonder if a nanny or maid had done it.

'Oh, nothing. I'm being silly. All this death in the family is getting to me. First Father and now Aunt Veronica. You ask if Father was the type to take his own life. I have to ask you, was Aunt Veronica? Because she always seemed so cheerful in her letters to me.'

'She was a cheerful woman,' said Sheila. 'But . . . '

'We had a lot of debt,' Peg finished for her. 'Father's death duties and other things. She may have been more worried than she let on.' Even as Peg said the words, it did not make sense. 'Perhaps your father's death upset her more than we know. Were they especially close?'

Cassie shrugged her delicate shoulders. 'Not as far as I know. I was the one who kept in touch with Aunt Veronica, first of all at my mother's insistence and then because I wanted to. She told me all about you two, you know, when she married your father. How she hoped she would be a good mother to you both. Then later . . . ' Cassie coughed discreetly.

'We . . . I . . . wasn't always very nice to her,' Peg admitted. 'It was nothing personal. I'm not nice to lots of people. Sheila is. She's a darling, whereas I'm the devil himself.'

'No you're not,' said Sheila. 'Well, not always.'

'She still cared about you both,' said Cassie. 'She worried, after your father died, that she could not do right by you.'

'Did she?' Peg felt a tingling in the back of her neck that she recognised as guilt. She had given Veronica a hard time. No wonder Mary was so angry with her. 'If you two don't mind, I think I'll turn in. Leave you to talk about fashions and men and all that.'

As she was leaving the drawing room, she heard Cassie say, 'Tell me all about Doctor Pearson. Is he married?'

Pity, thought Peg, *and just as I'm starting to like Cassie Harrington*.

On the way to her room, Peg stopped by Mary's door, which was ajar. Her little sister was lying in bed with her eyes open.

'Can I get you anything, darling?' Peg asked.

'No.'

Peg pushed the door open and went in. 'Mary, I know you're angry with me, but I never meant any harm to Veronica. She gave as good as she got, you know.'

'It's not that,' said Mary, her eyes filling with tears. 'I'm not mad at you anymore.'

'Then what is it, baby?' Peg sat on the edge of the bed and took Mary's hand. It was freezing cold. Instinctively, she wrapped it in both of hers and pressed it against her torso to warm it up.

'She left me, Peg. She left me. How could she do that?'

It was a question that Peg had asked herself. Veronica might not have cared much for Peg and Sheila — although Cassie's revelation about the letters suggested otherwise — but she adored Mary. 'I don't know, sweetheart. I really don't know.'

'Peg?'

'What, darling?'

'You're good at finding out things, aren't you?'

'I suppose so.'

'Then please find out who killed

Mummy, because I really don't think she would have left me.' Sobs racked Mary's body. Peg lifted her up to her, cradling her in her arms. 'Please, Peg.'

'All right, I will try to find out. But you might have to accept the truth, baby, no matter how painful. And that is that Mummy took an overdose of laudanum, because she was desperately worried.' Peg knew that Sheila would have been angry if she heard Peg say it so bluntly to Mary, but Peg did not believe in candy-coating bad news. Besides, Mary would know the truth soon enough, and it was better that she heard it from the people who loved and cared about her than a cruel and unthinking villager.

'I will. I promise. I do love you, Peg, even though you can be grumpy sometimes.'

'I love you, my sweet girl. And whatever happens, I promise I will never leave you.'

* * *

Cassie's dream of Helen was always the same, but details had become stronger since she came to England, as if memories were being awoken. They were in the garden and the two little girls were holding hands, and looking for somewhere to hide.

'Quickly, before she finds us,' Helen cried, her little face a mask of pain and fear. 'If she finds us . . . '

Helen did not have to tell Cassie about the consequences. They found an old outhouse on the edge of the garden, leading into the woods. Any other time they might have been afraid to go in there, but her mother's wrath was even more terrifying. There was an old sofa in the outhouse, so they hid behind that, clinging together.

The door to the outhouse opened and a woman entered. 'Cassie,' a gentle voice said. Receiving no answer, the woman went out again.

'She's only pretending to be nice,' Helen whispered. 'That's what they do. They act nice and then they hurt you.'

Cassie gulped, then looked down to see that she had wet herself. Her humiliation was complete.

She awoke, a grown woman, with tears streaming down her face. She wished she had never come back to Midchester. It held too many painful memories, some of which she could not trust.

★ ★ ★

A day or two later, Peg called up at Bedlington Hall to see Gerry Sanderson. 'How do you fancy a trip out?' she asked. 'I've borrowed a car from the garage here, and as everything belongs to you now, no one can say I've stolen it. Unless you're going to drop me in it.'

'Where are we going with my car?' asked Gerry with a grin.

'According to everyone else, I'm just helping you to get out and about as part of your recuperation. In reality, we're off to Shrewsbury, to the hotel where Veronica was found. I have a commission to solve a crime.'

'Really? Who from? The beautiful Miss Harrington?'

'No, it's from the even more beautiful Miss Bradbourne.' She was not too happy with Gerry's puzzled frown. He could have pretended it was her. 'I mean Mary, you fool,' she said.

'Are you sure that's wise, Peg? The poor kid's been through enough.'

'She asked me to find out the truth, so that's what I'm going to do. I don't do much for other people, but for Mary I'd walk over hot coals.'

He nodded, with understanding in his eyes. 'I know you would, old girl. Come on then, let's go and solve a mystery together!'

Despite being stung by the 'old girl' comment, Peg thought that driving through the countryside with Gerry was more fun than it should have been under the circumstances. With the top down and the sun shining above them, it was hard to believe that there had been so much tragedy in the preceding weeks. It was also hard to believe that hundreds of miles away, young men were fighting for their lives in dirty, rat infested trenches. Even with Bedlington Hall being given over to the military and the new aerodrome just outside Midchester, the war seemed a long way away.

'Wait till I tell Freddie about this,' she said with a smile as they neared their destination. 'He loves a mystery.'

'Must you?' Gerry said, becoming serious.

'Whyever not?'

'Oh, I just wonder if he'll be very happy about me running around with his sister. Some fellows can get funny about it, you know.'

'You're not one of Freddie's special friends, are you?' Peg asked, then immediately wished she had not.

'Special friends?'

'Oh you know, fire-forged friends and all that,' she said, to cover up her gaffe.

'We have seen a lot of action together, of course, but no, that's not it. I'd just rather if you didn't mention me. It can be hard for the fellows out there to hear about those of us who made it home, that's all. I don't want to make him too wistful.'

Peg did not understand that at all. From her own experience of writing to her brother, he liked to hear of even the

93

most trivial events at home. 'Oh well, if you'd rather I didn't, then I won't. Besides, I'll have enough bad news to tell him.'

They were quiet for the rest of the trip, but Peg told herself it was a comfortable silence, even though she sensed that Gerry's thoughts were not exactly with her. Still, he was there, and he seemed to enjoy her company.

The hotel was in a tiny back alley in the centre of Shrewsbury. The lace curtains on the window might have been white once, but they had become yellow with age. When Peg and Gerry walked in through the door, the man on the desk smirked and said, 'Mr and Mrs Smith, I presume.' He was a sweaty-looking man, wearing a shirt which had a dirty collar.

'Actually it's Miss Bradbourne and Mr Sanderson.'

'Now, miss,' the man said with a note of caution. 'Let's be discreet, shall we? I don't want the authorities to close me down.'

'Does my name mean nothing to you?' Peg asked.

'Should it?'

'My stepmother, Veronica Bradbourne, was found dead in one of your rooms last week. She committed suicide. It's hardly something you'd forget.'

'Shh . . . ' The man came from behind the desk and shut the door leading into the lounge. 'I've got a business to run and there's some people as wouldn't like to hear that.'

'I'd like to ask you some questions,' said Peg.

'I already told the police all I know.'

'There's money in it for you,' said Gerry, reaching into his pocket. He turned to Peg. 'Except I forgot my wallet.'

'Luckily I was paid this morning,' she sighed. 'As Mr Sanderson said, there's money in it for you. I'd also like to see the room, if that's possible.'

'It's erm . . . taken at the moment.'

'I'm sure it will be free within the hour,' Gerry said wryly.

'What do you mean?' asked Peg.

'Well, erm . . . Never mind. We'll wait, Mr — ?'

'Jones.'

Peg doubted Jones was any more the man's name than Smith was hers and Gerry's, but she let it go. 'Okay, I'll just ask questions. Do you remember my stepmother coming in?' she asked.

'Yes, I do, miss,' Jones said. His voice was more respectful, seemingly having realised he was talking to a lady rather than an easy girl needing a sleazy room for herself and her lover. 'She was a bit too rich for this place, to be honest, but she seemed very happy and excited to be here.'

'So she did not seem downhearted?' asked Peg.

'Not that I could see. I told the police that. Whether it was an act, I don't know, miss. But she seemed happy enough to me.'

'Did you see the man she was supposed to meet?'

'I can't say I did, miss. At least no one came in and asked for her. I went off duty at around six.'

'It was days before she was found, wasn't it?'

'Well, yes, miss, because she booked the

room for several days. When the maid tried to go in, the door was locked and there was a 'do not disturb' sign on the door, so well . . . we assumed she wanted some privacy. Same as most of our clientele. It was only when . . . ' He paused. 'Well, we realised something was wrong.'

'The smell,' said Peg.

'Yes, miss. The smell.'

'Who else stayed whilst she was here?'

'I'm afraid I can't answer that, miss.'

'I realise you have to be discreet.'

'No, miss — I mean, I can't answer. As you've probably realised, no one gives their real names here, so I honestly couldn't tell you. Well, except Mrs Bradbourne, and until they found her, I assumed that was a false name. You could have knocked me down with a feather when it turned out be her real name.'

'If she wasn't meeting a man, why would she come here, Gerry?' She turned to her friend.

'It doesn't make sense, does it? Not a nice lady like that, in a place like this. Sorry,' Gerry said to Jones. 'No offence meant.'

'None taken, sir. I know what type of place I run, but it makes money you see, especially during a war. Besides, why shouldn't people have a bit of happiness when so many young men are dying out there?'

His argument was irrefutable as far as Peg could see. 'Could you describe any of the other people who were here?' she asked. 'We're looking for a man about six feet tall, with dark hair.'

'That describes lots of men, miss.'

'He drives a bullnose Morris Crowley.'

'Now wait, that does sound familiar. There's not many of them around here.'

'No, there aren't.'

'I'm not saying he comes here, mind you. He'd not thank me for saying that. But his name is Alexander Marshall. He's a marquis or an earl or something, but he's one of those socialists, so he's dropped his title. He lives somewhere out towards Midchester. In one of those little hamlets. Just fancies himself as an artist, I think, so he's got a studio.'

'Thank you!' said Peg. 'Now, may we see the room?'

It was another half hour before they could see the room. The bed had not even been made. Peg blushed to think of what had happened there. She also wondered at people who could find any kind of romance, even the sleazy kind, in a bedroom where someone had died.

It was a miserable little room, with dark stained wallpaper and a lumpy-looking bed with sheets that looked as if they needed a good boil. Or perhaps to be burned to cinders, Peg thought.

'What do you hope to find, Peg?' asked Gerry.

'I have absolutely no idea, to be honest,' she said. 'I suppose the police have found everything they needed to find. I just wondered if Veronica had left anything here. Something that might give a clue as to her state of mind or who she met.'

'Actually,' said Jones, 'there was something the maid found afterwards. I meant to tell the police, but I've been a bit busy.' He looked sheepish.

'You mean she took it,' said Peg.

'She's an honest girl, is Myrtle. But

sometimes things drop into the mop bucket.'

Peg imagined they did, and wondered why Jones was admitting it now. 'What is it?'

Jones went away and came back a few minutes later. 'It's this brooch.' He handed it to Peg. It was the blue lapis lazuli brooch that Veronica had been wearing when she went out with the man in the car. 'Myrtle said she was wearing it when she arrived,' Jones explained, 'and that she found it on the floor, just outside the bedroom door. She meant to give it to me, she says, but we were busy what with the police running around. Anyway, you've got it now.'

'He probably thought we knew about it,' said Peg, as she and Gerry drove back to Midchester. 'And that we'd missed it in amongst her personal effects.'

'Yes, that's what I think. His giving it back to you was damage limitation to stop you sending the police around. I think Mr Jones is probably into a lot of things he wouldn't thank the police for knowing.'

'What makes you say that?'

'That hotel must be running at a loss, because no decent person would go there, yet he keeps it open. It'll be a front for something. The black market, maybe. Young Myrtle probably found the brooch and handed it in as the dutiful young maid she is, but he realised he couldn't shift it. Not with the way Veronica died in his place.'

'Goodness, dear cousin. You do know a lot about crime.'

'There was a man in our unit. Name of Harry Carter. What he didn't know about crime wasn't worth knowing. He was a handy man to have around when we ran short of food and drink, but not the sort of man that you'd want to take home to Mother.' Gerry's voice was grim.

'It sounds as if you didn't much like him.'

'War makes for strange bedfellows.'

'Now we need to find out where this earl-turned-socialist artist Alexander Marshall lives and go and question him.'

'Peg, dear girl. Don't you think you should leave this to the police now?'

'No, I told Mary I'd do it. Archer is a good man, and good at his job. But I think we — I — could probably get people to open up a bit more. To all intents and purposes, Veronica committed suicide and as far as anyone knows, I'm just trying to find out why. If Archer gets involved, word will get around that it's a murder investigation and they'll clam up.'

Peg stopped at the local police station on her way home. The place was a hive of activity. 'Constable Archer,' she said, when he came from the back room where the cells were situated. 'I have some information for you. The man my stepmother was seeing might have been a man called Alexander Marshall. Do you know him?'

'I know of him, miss, but we've got other problems at the moment.' He turned to the young policeman who was sitting behind the counter. 'Come with me, Simpson.'

'You need to go and speak to Marshall,' Peg insisted. 'Please, Constable Archer.'

'Miss Bradbourne, I know you're distressed about your stepmother, but we've got a lead in the Arthur Harrington case. If we don't hurry, that lead may get on a train to London and we may never find him again.'

'Who? Harrington committed suicide, didn't he?'

'Yes, but he also lost his boots. And guess who has just taken delivery of a new pair of boots.'

'Colonel Trent. I saw him in them the other day.'

Archer's lips twisted into a grin. 'You spinster sleuths and the way you insist on keeping things to yourselves. Yes, it's Colonel Trent, and I'm going to find out exactly how he came by his new boots.'

'May I accompany you?'

'You most certainly may not. We don't work that way, Miss Bradbourne, no matter how they do it in books.'

Peg could only watch in frustration as Archer and his men left the police station.

8

'If you could just tell us where you got the boots, Colonel, we can clear all this up,' Archer said. They spoke to Colonel Trent in his own sitting room, rather than embarrassing him by taking him to the police station. But that did not stop the women on Spinsters' Row from standing at their gates, gossiping about the police visit.

'Good people should not have to deal with the police,' said Miss Cartwright. 'And I am sure the colonel is a good man. Not that he isn't a bit sharp from time to time. Why, only the other day . . . '

As she regaled her listeners with a story of the colonel's grumpiness when she asked for advice on her roses, Archer took a more discreet approach. 'It wouldn't be the first time a man bought something from someone at the pub,' he suggested.

'I do not frequent that establishment,' said the colonel. 'And nor would I.'

'There's nothing wrong with the Quiet Woman,' said Archer. 'It's a very respectable establishment, run by my brother-in-law.'

'You wouldn't say that if you knew . . . ' The colonel clamped his lips shut. With his spine rigid in a high-back leather seat that had seen better days, it looked as if he were the one sitting in judgement. 'A man should be able to buy a new pair of boots without being accused of murder.'

'No one is accusing you of murder, Colonel Trent. It is without doubt that Doctor Harrington took his own life. But his boots were missing, and suddenly you have a new pair. Only the other day I noticed there were holes in your gardening boots.'

'Which is a very good reason for my buying a new pair, would you not say?'

'Colonel Trent, the boots you are wearing are very expensive. Now . . . ' Archer lowered his eyes respectfully. 'I know you are not a rich man. Plus . . . well, they're American-made.'

'Do we not have importers and exporters of goods in Britain?' the colonel asked, his face reddening.

'We do, in which case those boots would cost even more. Now there are no charges against you, Colonel, and nor will there be. You bought them in good faith. I just need to know where you got them. You said something about the pub and how I wouldn't call it respectable if I knew. If I knew what? Are you suggesting that Frank Yeardley sold them to you?'

'I most certainly am not. Mr Yeardley may not be my type of person, but I gather he is an honest man.' Whatever failings Colonel Trent might have, he could not be anything but honest about a fellow human being.

'His son then?'

'It's more the company he keeps,' said the colonel. 'You say I am not to be charged.'

'There will be no charge, though we will have to take the boots as evidence.'

The colonel let out a big sigh. 'It was young Fletcher. Percy, I think they call him. He sold them to me. I didn't realise they were from a dead man. I didn't ask. I suppose I didn't want to know. But if you say they're Harrington's then they must be.'

'So Percy didn't tell you how he came by them?'

'No. As I said, I didn't ask. Well one doesn't, does one? And now I suppose I shall have to just mend my old pair.'

Constable Archer looked at the old colonel, his warm eyes full of sympathy. 'Actually, I have a pair that were given to me as part of my uniform, but they were a size too big. I'd be happy to let you have them if they're the right size.'

'I'm a size ten . . . ' The colonel remembered his pride, adding, 'I don't need charity.'

'Of course not, and I wouldn't offer it. I'll bring them over and you pay me when you're ready. It doesn't have to be this week.' He had no such boots either, but there were some at the station left behind by the younger constables who had enlisted. At least they would be put to good use. Someone had to look after the men who came back from the wars to an ungrateful country. If the current war ever came to an end there would be even more of them scraping a living, but Archer would worry about that when the time came.

When he left Colonel Trent's house, he went to the pub, looking for Tom Yeardley.

'He's not here,' said Frank, when Archer reached the pub. Peg and Gerry Sanderson were in there, having a drink. 'He went off out this morning and I haven't seen him since. I don't know what's happening with that boy, honestly I don't, Bert.'

'Have you seen Percy Fletcher then, Frank? He's the one I really need to see.'

'Why, what's he been up to?'

'Selling stolen boots to Colonel Trent. They belonged to Doctor Harrington.'

'That's a rum business, isn't it? Fancy the doctor coming back after all these years. I'm glad my Milly wasn't here to see him. It would have cut her up something rotten.'

'Why's that then?'

'Well you know that my Milly and her sister, Tilly, used to come up from down south for the strawberry-picking?'

'Yes.'

'Tilly and the doctor had a fling. She was a bit of a lass, was Tilly. Not like my Milly. She already had a kid.'

'Milly?'

Frank rolled his eyes. 'No, Tilly. She had a little girl, Helen, by some bloke she met down south. Used to drag the poor little thing around everywhere. More often than not, Milly ended up looking after Helen. She loved that little girl. Then when Harrington finished with Tilly — they had a row, right here in the middle of the street — she went off, taking Helen with her. It was a couple of years before you moved from Hereford and married our Adeline.'

'That explains why I don't remember it.'

'Broke Milly's heart, it did,' said Frank as he wiped the bar over with a damp cloth. 'She said she ought to have been that child's mother. She had one letter from Tilly, saying she'd found work in Portsmouth, but that was it. Anyway, the next summer, when Milly came back up for the strawberry-picking, we got married and she stayed here until . . . well you know. She was the best woman in the world, my Milly. Worth two of that bloody sister of hers.'

'Was Tilly the only one Harrington ran around with?'

'No, Bert. He was said to have women all over the place. He even tried wooing Miss Cartwright till he realised she was poor as a church mouse. Mind you, it brought a happy blush to the old woman's cheeks. It's a wonder Miss Penelope had owt to do with him, but he was a handsome sort, and she had money from her uncle. That was a strange thing. The uncle left Veronica Bradbourne out of his will completely. They say there was something funny about it. You know, that he had an 'interest' in Penelope. The dodgy uncle type of interest, but she was no oil painting. Veronica got the looks, but Penelope got the money. There was something a bit wanting about that girl.'

'Penelope Harrington?'

'Yeah. She was nice enough, but prone to madness. Rumour had it that the doctor didn't like leaving her alone with the child. It ran in the family, by all accounts. Insanity.'

'Her daughter seems sane enough,' Peg piped up. She had been listening avidly to the conversation.

'Did you actually just say something nice about Cassie Harrington?' Gerry teased.

'I was about to add 'in a dumb American' way,' Peg said waspishly. 'But no, she's not dumb. In fact, I think she's probably rather clever. She's certainly wrapped Gerry and Doctor Pearson around her little finger with her little-girl-lost act.'

'If you see your Tom, tell him I'd like a word please, Frank,' said Archer, grinning. He bid Peg and Gerry good day.

'Aren't you going to tell him about the brooch?' Gerry muttered to Peg as Frank went about his business behind the bar.

'No, he'll only want to put it in evidence, and I think Mary should have it. Anyway, it serves him right for giving me what-for about keeping evidence to myself.'

Peg finished her bottle of stout and returned home. Sheila, Mary and Cassie Harrington were in the sitting room, taking afternoon tea. 'Mary, darling,' said Peg. 'I found something for you today.

Something of Veronica's I thought you might like to have.' She took the lapis lazuli brooch out of her pocket and gave it to her little sister. Mary frowned. 'What's wrong? Don't you like it?'

Before Mary could answer, Cassie Harrington managed to drop her tea cup, breaking it in two.

9

Cassie looked up at the old doctor's surgery. Despite the heat from the mid-day sun, she was shivering inside. The house was somehow strange and familiar. It had been her home, and yet she felt no affinity with it. She had thought that once she arrived in Midchester, the past would open up to her, helping to clear up some of the confused memories and dreams that she had experienced since moving to America.

She did not want to go inside, feeling that she had no real right to be there, so she walked around the garden, which had become overgrown through lack of care. The effect was rather attractive, with wildflowers swaying in the gentle breeze.

Around the back was the outhouse that often appeared in her dreams, but the roof had fallen in, and looking through the window, she could see that the old sofa was more frayed and busted than it had been when she and her little friend had hidden there. She could still hear Helen's voice talking about how one could not trust adults, even when they were being nice to you. It was a harsh lesson Cassie had learned, to the point that leaving for boarding school was one of the happiest moments of her life. Yet there had been kindness back then, in Midchester. She could not remember it clearly, but it was there. A warm smile and a soft hand, soothing her. The vague memory brought tears to her eyes.

She was startled out of her reverie by a voice saying, 'Hello there.'

'Oh.'

'I'm sorry,' said Doctor Pearson. 'I didn't mean to startle you. I was visiting a lady on Spinsters' Row when I saw you walking past. It occurred to me that perhaps you should not be up here alone.'

'I am able to take care of myself, Doctor Pearson.'

'Of course. I didn't mean to intrude.' He turned to go.

'Please, don't go. I apologise. It's just that seeing the old place has rattled me.

I'm glad you're here, as I wanted to go inside, but I did not want to be alone.'

'Are you sure that's wise? This place holds only sadness for you now, surely.'

'I'm not sure what it holds. I barely recognise it as the place I used to live.'

'You were very young at the time.'

'Yes, that's true. Would you come inside with me? I'd like to see where . . . ' Her voice tailed off.

'If you're certain,' said Pearson. 'I wouldn't want to upset you. You seem sad enough as it is.'

She swallowed hard. 'Yes, I'm sure. I think.'

They walked back around to the front of the house, due to the French windows and back door being impassable, because of the foliage that had grown up around them. Ivy completely covered the back of the house.

'Nature always takes back in the end,' Pearson said.

'Yes, I suppose it does,' said Cassie with a wan smile.

'What's it like in America? I've always fancied going there.'

'New York is a wonderful city,' said Cassie. 'It's growing all the time. Buildings so high you think you could reach God if you went right to the top of them. Central Park is beautiful at this time of year.'

'You miss it?'

'Yes, I do. It's my home and for the most part I've been happy there.'

'For the most part?'

'Mother can be . . . changeable.'

'Tell me about it. My own mother is a bit of a harridan. When is your mother coming to Midchester?'

'I don't know. She isn't keen to come back here at all. I think she and Father had problems here, and that's why they left. She says it wasn't a happy place for her. Father . . . ' She paused. 'Oh I don't suppose it matters what I tell you now that he's dead. Father had a wandering eye.'

'I see.'

'I think they left Midchester because he had an affair. I imagine in a small place like this, it's hard to hide. I don't know if he was always faithful to mother in New

116

York, but it's a big place, so maybe he got better at hiding it.'

They reached the front door, and Andrew pushed it open. It scraped on the floor, damp having swelled the wood.

'So what do you remember?' he asked.

Cassie stood in the hallway, looking up at the rickety staircase, then to the drawing room on one side and the dining room on the other. Another gap, where there used to be a door, led into the kitchen. She could see the remnants of an old stove through the door. Yet another door, behind the staircase, was shut tight. 'I think that was the surgery,' she said. She moved to the drawing room. 'That's right. There's another door leading from it there. I remember that. I remember father checking my tonsils. Ha . . . ' She did not laugh so much as emit a small sound of triumph. 'I had forgotten that, but yes, I suffered with tonsillitis. And Mother brought me . . . ' She faltered and laughed. 'No, she wouldn't have brought me, would she? We'd already be here. How silly of me.'

'I like your laughter,' said Pearson. 'You

bring real sunshine to this dull place, Miss Harrington.'

She rewarded him with a warm smile, but it did not last long. 'Can we go upstairs now?'

'Miss Harrington . . . '

'Please, call me Cassie. I should really like to go upstairs, Doctor Pearson. It's not as if Father is still there.'

He helped her to traverse the dangerous staircase and she went straight to the nursery. 'I remember this room!' she cried. 'Yes, I do. Helen and I used to sleep here.'

'Helen?'

'My little friend. And I'm afraid that's as much as I can remember.'

She walked over to the wall where her height had been recorded. 'I don't remember this,' she said. 'But it must have happened. Only I don't know who did it.'

'Your mother or father?'

'I doubt it, Doctor Pearson . . . '

'Call me Andrew.'

'Andrew. I doubt it very much. I don't remember either of my parents being that

118

interested in me. When I came top of my class at boarding school, Father's reaction was one of surprise and Mother asked me if I'd cheated.' She sighed. 'Yet I had a feeling of being loved in this house. Earlier, just before you arrived. There was kindness and gentleness. But it can't have been either my father or my mother. Oh, my father wasn't particularly unkind. Indifferent is a better word. Sometimes I think he forgot I existed. But my mother . . . ' Her eyes became downcast. 'Let's not talk about such things. Being in this place is making me melancholy. I miss something — someone — only I'm not sure what it is that I miss. Isn't that strange?'

'We've a tendency to think that we were happier as children, with no cares and no worries. Sometimes that's true.'

'I wonder why he came here to die,' she mused, taking a last walk around the nursery. 'Why in this house? In this room?'

'Perhaps he was happy here,' Pearson suggested. 'And that's what you remember.'

'Perhaps.' She shivered again. 'I think I've seen all I want to see, Andrew. Can we leave now?'

They walked back to the village in silence, with Cassie lost in thought. She had enjoyed her few days in Midchester. Sheila and Mary Bradbourne were charming, and whilst Peg could be strident, Cassie sensed no real harm in the girl. What she had really enjoyed was being without her mother. She began to think of a way she could make that state of affairs permanent.

10

Alexander Marshall lived in an old artisan cottage set amongst the area's rolling hills. A manservant, holding a boot in one hand and a brush in the other, opened the door and informed Peg and Gerry that Mr Marshall was in his studio at the bottom of the garden.

'I see that he still needs a valet-cum-butler, despite his socialist leanings,' Peg muttered to Gerry as they walked around to the back of the cottage.

'Rich people never really give up being rich,' Gerry said, with a note of bitterness in his voice.

'Would you give your newly inherited money away?' asked Peg.

'No chance. I've been broke all my life, so it's about time I had something.'

'Really? To be honest, you don't talk much about your life before you came here.'

'There's the studio,' said Gerry, pointing.

As the manservant had said, the studio was at the bottom of the garden. It was a wooden hut, rather ramshackle in design. Peg felt sure that one gust of wind would blow it right down.

'Mr Marshall,' Peg called. 'Are you there?'

She was not prepared for the man who opened the door. For a start, he only looked to be in his late twenties or early thirties, which would make him younger than Veronica. He was also devastatingly handsome, with thick dark hair and pale blue eyes. She felt her female heart flutter a little, but decided that being attracted to two men — Gerry Sanderson and Andrew Pearson — was quite enough for one year.

'How can I help you?' he asked. He wiped his hands onto his shirt, which was already covered in paint.

'My name is Peg — Margaret — Bradbourne.'

'You're Veronica's stepdaughter, aren't you? I meant to call on her but I've been rather busy. Does she want a decision about the house?'

'The house? Oh . . . then you don't know?'

'Don't know what?'

'May we come in?' Peg said, sure that Marshall's manservant was watching them. 'To speak to you privately?'

'Of course.'

When Peg entered Marshall's studio, it became obvious he had known Veronica. A portrait of her, wearing a flowing robe in the style of a Greek goddess, stood against one of the walls. The robe was held together with the lapis lazuli brooch that had been left at the hotel. It was as if Peg were seeing her stepmother through someone else's eyes, for she had never really given much thought to how beautiful Veronica was. Seeing this portrait made her realise why her father had wanted Veronica around. For an ailing, elderly man she must have been quite a tonic. If Peg were honest, Veronica had also been a good wife, never failing in her duty to care for William Bradbourne, despite the fact they had both entered into a marriage of convenience. Veronica gave William youth and he, in his turn,

123

had given her stability.

Other portraits showed Mr Marshall to be very talented indeed, if not adventurous. She guessed these were his bread and butter, as they were mostly portraits of people, and some family groups or pets. Some paintings were more experimental, clearly inspired by cubism, and were not quite to Peg's taste. Another set still was made up entirely of white feathers and red poppies. She wondered at the symbolism, and would have liked to discuss it with him, but had other things to worry about.

'She came to you to have her portrait painted,' Peg murmured.

'Yes, before your father died. She wanted to present it to him as a Christmas present. When he died, she decided it was not appropriate. I think she could not really afford it, which is why I offered to buy the house. Now, Miss Bradbourne. Will you tell me what's wrong?'

Peg, still fascinated by the portraits, turned to look at Alexander Marshall. 'Veronica is dead. She died a fortnight ago, only they didn't find her body straight away.'

'Good Lord!' Marshall was either a good actor or he was genuinely shocked by the news. 'But she was so young. How? What do you mean they didn't find her body? I'm sorry to ask so many questions. I am just so shocked by this news.'

'They say she took her own life, in a hotel in Shrewsbury.' Peg mentioned the name of the hotel and saw a glint of recognition in Marshall's eyes. Mr Jones, the manager, had been right. 'You do know it?'

'Most single men of my age do,' said Marshall, grinning slightly. 'In fact, Veronica telephoned me to ask if I knew of a discreet place she could meet someone. I told her the name of the hotel.'

'Did she tell you who she was going to meet?' asked Peg.

Marshall shook his head. 'No, but she sounded very happy and excited.'

'I have to be honest here, Mr Marshall,' Peg said. 'And tell you that I thought she had gone there to meet you. I saw you together driving away from our house and I saw the way she looked at you.'

'I promise you that whatever interest Veronica had in me was not requited. Yes, she was a very beautiful and charming woman, but I was only interested in her from an artist's point of view, and then when I saw the house I realised I could help her. It's a wonderful old house. I gather it used to be a priory.'

'Yes, that's right.'

'And you're still going to sell?'

'As soon as we've got over grieving for Veronica, yes,' Peg said sharply. She knew she was being unfair, as though she regretted Veronica's death, she could not really say she had grieved.

'Forgive me; I didn't mean to sound callous. But I do want that house, and I imagine your tax problems are going to be even greater now that Veronica is dead. I could help you. I'm happy to help you.'

'I'll discuss it with my sister Sheila and get back to you,' said Peg, calming down.

'So you definitely weren't at the hotel with Veronica,' Gerry cut in, sounding peeved.

'No, certainly not.'

'Do you have an alibi?' asked Gerry.

'Gerry!' Peg exclaimed.

'Sorry.'

Marshall looked from Gerry to Peg and back again before smiling. 'As I don't know what day she died, I can't say if I have an alibi or not.'

'None of us really know,' Peg admitted. 'She had been dead several days when they found her, and she left our home on the Saturday morning after being seen alive by our maid, Izzy. But other than that, we don't know the exact day that she died.'

'It's a dreadful thing to happen,' Marshall said. He crossed his arms and then put one hand to his chin, as if ruminating on the meaning of life and death.

'And you're sure you don't know who she was going to meet?' asked Peg.

'I'm afraid I don't. Whatever you may think of the relationship between your stepmother and me, it was purely business. First for the portrait and then because I wanted to buy the house. I imagine that when you saw us, I was taking her out to tea in order to make an offer.'

'Thank you,' said Peg. 'I'm sorry we've taken up your time, but I should warn you that I've given your name to the police.'

'Yes, they've already been around.'

'Have they? In that case, I apologise for bothering you.' Peg made her way to the door, followed by Gerry. She nearly bumped into him when she turned back. 'Mr Marshall?'

'Yes, Miss Bradbourne.'

'About the portrait. How much did Veronica owe you for it?'

'Twenty pounds.'

'Oh, I see.' Peg did not have that amount of money hanging around. She could use her savings, but they were meagre enough. 'The thing is, I think my sister Mary might like it, as a memento of her mother. I don't suppose you'd consider accepting fifteen pounds?'

'I'll tell you what, Miss Bradbourne. You take the picture for young Mary and tell her it's a gift from a man who admired her mother greatly.'

Peg felt tears sting her eyes. She had always been awful to Veronica, and it never occurred to her that others might admire her stepmother. Peg had never given Veronica enough credit for dealing with two stepdaughters, one of whom could be very difficult, and her own child. 'She will be very glad to hear it. Thank you.'

'And do get in touch when you're ready to sell the house.'

Peg nodded, guessing that his kind gesture had more to do with his interest in the house than any genuine feelings of sympathy for Mary. But it did not matter, as long as Peg had the portrait for her sister.

'That was very good of him,' Peg said to Gerry as she drove them back to Midchester, with the portrait in the back seat of the car.

'Hmm,' said Gerry.

'What? Don't you think it was kind?' Even though Peg had her own suspicions about Marshall's motives in letting her have the portrait, it irked her that Gerry seemed to share them. She would rather be told she was wrong.

'He can afford it,' Gerry said. 'Men like that who claim to give up their titles, but still have a manservant and can think of buying a house with little thought of cost . . . they make me sick. My guess is that he gave up his title, but not the money that Daddy left him. He hasn't really had to earn a day's wage in his life and when he's tired of painting portraits of spoiled socialites, he'll find some other hobby to pretend he's a working man.'

'Says a man who has just inherited a vast estate!' Peg snapped. 'What's wrong, Gerry? Are you jealous of him?'

'Well you clearly liked the handsome devil.'

Peg laughed, delighted. 'You are jealous! Well don't worry. The likes of Mr Marshall are not for a plain girl like me.'

'You're not plain, Peg. You're lovely.'

'That's very sweet of you to say so, Gerry.'

'No, really. You're lovely and if things were different . . . ' He paused.

Peg took her eyes off the road briefly.

The car swerved and she fought to bring it back under control. 'What do you mean?'

'Nothing, Peg. Let's just enjoy the time we spend together, hey? I like being with you. You're not like the others of your class.'

Peg frowned. 'Says the current heir of Bedlington Hall.'

'Yes, I am aren't I? Strange, I keep forgetting that. I've spent so much of my life with nothing, I can't quite conceive of having so much.'

'So what did you do, before you inherited the estate?'

'I was in the army, of course.'

'I mean before that. Before the war started. What did you do?'

'A bit of this. A bit of that. You know. Selling used cars. Door-to-door salesman.'

'It's strange, but it never occurs to me that when an estate is entailed away it can go to anyone in the family line, even if he is a dustman. But your mother was the daughter of the last Lord Bedlington, wasn't she?'

'Yes. But we weren't rich. Er . . . most of the money went on caring for my father, and my mother was too proud to claim off the family estate, even though there was no one else it could go to. There weren't any Bedlingtons left. She and old Lady Bedlington, her stepmother, didn't get on most of the time. It was only after my mother died that I decided to claim what was mine.'

'Oh yes, of course. Your father was sick, wasn't he?'

'Completely mental.'

'Poor man. I heard he was locked up by mistake, but then it made him mad anyway.'

'Who told you that?'

'My mother and father. They knew your parents before they moved to India. Your father's brother was murdered right here in Midchester. Mama worked out who the killer was. Father said she was incredible, and saved him from the gallows.'

'How romantic.'

'I always thought so,' said Peg, feeling that Gerry was making fun of her.

'No, really it is. She must have really believed in him.'

'She did.'

'Do you believe in me, Peg? If push came to shove, would you stand by me?'

Peg answered carefully, afraid of letting her feelings show. 'I hope I always stand by my friends, Gerry.'

'That's all we are?'

'That's what you said, wasn't it? About enjoying our time together.'

'Yes, of course. And I meant it. You're a very special woman, Peg. Sometimes I don't think you actually believe it, which is why you're so sharp with people.'

'I'm not special at all. Sheila is special and Mary is special. I'm . . . oh I don't know. Sometimes I feel as if I got into this family by mistake. Mother used to call me her changeling, because I was always angry as a child, whereas Sheila was so placid and well-behaved. She — Mother — would hold me tight when I had my tantrums, and tell me over and over that it didn't matter how angry I got, she would always love me.' A tear rolled down Peg's cheek, remembering her gentle mother and how much trouble Peg had caused her. 'I think she thought it helped, but it didn't, because I got to thinking that she and Father only made allowances for me. Sheila is the same. She'll tell me she loves me, and then comes the 'but' . . . '

'I think you're being hard on yourself and on them,' said Gerry.

'Do you?'

'Yes. Because what they're saying is that they love you unconditionally. You're lucky to get that, Peg. Some people wait all their lives to be accepted for what they are. You had it from the very beginning.'

'Did I? Yes, I suppose I did. I'd never thought of it like that. And now you've done that thing again where we start off talking about you and it ends up about me.'

Gerry smiled. 'It makes sense. I'm boring. You're not.'

But there was more to it than that. For a man who had inherited a fortune, Gerry was surprisingly bitter about the upper classes. Perhaps it was because he had gone so long without, due to his mother's pride, but that was not it. There had been a strange light in his eyes as he spoke, full of darkness and hatred.

Maybe he was as mad as his father . . .

11

The two couples met in the market square, just outside the Quiet Woman pub. Pearson tipped his hat to Peg, and Gerry did the same to Carrie.

'Nice day,' said Pearson, coughing awkwardly.

'Yes, perfect for a walk,' said Peg politely. Inside she tried not to seethe. After all, why shouldn't Doctor Pearson walk in the sunshine with a beautiful young woman? She was with Gerry, and had noticed that when she was in Sanderson's company, she did not think of Pearson. Yet seeing the doctor with Cassie caused an ache she could not account for. 'Have you been walking in the hills?'

'No,' said Cassie. For the first time, Peg noticed the girl looked pale. 'I wanted to see where my father died.'

'Oh . . . I'm sorry. That must have been hard for you.'

'Yes, but I'm glad I did. So much of my early life is a blur. I can't say things are any clearer, but I remembered some things.'

'Such as what?' asked Peg.

'Hiding in the outhouse from my mother!'

'I've heard . . . ' Peg paused. She had heard the rumours about Penelope's mental state, but she felt awkward mentioning it, which was odd, considering how blunt she had been about Gerry's father. The situation with the two men seemed to be affecting her in ways she could not understand. If she behaved brusquely with Cassie, Pearson would know she was bothered. Not that it had worried her before. Things had changed. Before, he had only been attracted to a girl who was a stranger, and therefore seemed exotic to the inhabitants of Midchester. There was something else in Pearson's eyes now: a protectiveness that could only come from a man who was falling in love.

'You were saying?' said Cassie, looking Peg squarely in the eyes.

'I've heard that your mother was unwell. Please don't worry about it. Poor Gerry's father was a complete madman! Oh . . . ' Peg looked at Gerry, but to her surprise he was laughing.

'Honestly, Peg,' he joshed. 'Your milk of human kindness is a bit on the sour side sometimes.'

'I don't mean to be unkind,' Peg said, feeling bristling on the back of her neck and a flush in her cheeks. 'I just say what I think, hurt or offend.'

'Do you think that's right?' asked Pearson. He looked more annoyed than Gerry.

'To tell the truth? Of course I do.'

'Has it occurred to you that your truth might be different to someone else's, Miss Bradbourne?'

'Well I . . . ' She wanted to run away and hide, but Peg was no coward. 'I apologise, Cassie, Gerry. My mouth does rather run away with me sometimes.'

'There's no need to apologise,' Cassie said gently. She patted Peg on the arm. 'You've been very kind to me, even though I know it must be an imposition to have me in your home at such a dreadful time.'

'Actually it was Sheila's idea, but thank you. It's a much worse time for you, I'm sure.'

'Peg is an original,' said Gerry, his eyes twinkling. 'She's one of the chaps. And I wouldn't want to change one bit of her.'

'No, me neither,' said Pearson, placated. 'Midchester needs characters like Peg.'

Rather than be mollified, Peg was seething. They might think they were being kind, but she neither wanted to be 'one of the chaps' or a 'character'. She wanted to be like Cassie Harrington; the sort of girl that men fell hopelessly in love with after one meeting. The silly dreams she had about Gerry liking her as more than just a friend burst like a party balloon.

She was struggling with what to say when they heard an almighty screech coming from the train station. A train had ground to a halt just along the track.

'What on earth?' said Pearson. He quickly became professional and ran towards the station. Peg, Gerry and Cassie followed him, curious as to what had happened. Other villagers came out to do the same.

'A young lad fallen onto the tracks,' said one of the guards, running along the platform. 'Fetch the police and a doctor.'

'What lad?' said a voice from somewhere behind Peg. 'Is it my Tom? Is it?'

Frank Yeardley dashed forward, his face pale and terrified. 'He's been missing for days. Is it my Tom?'

'Now, Frank,' said Constable Archer, who had come to take control of the situation. 'We've been looking for Tom discreetly, just as you asked us to. There's no evidence that he was still in Midchester.'

'I have to go and see. I have to know.' Before anyone could stop him, Frank dashed past the guard and towards the end of the platform. He jumped down, ignoring the shouts of the guards.

'Frank, come on,' said Archer, chasing him. He turned back to Peg. 'He doesn't want to see this if it is.' He held up his hand when Peg and the others went to follow. 'No, stay back. No one needs to see this.' Only Andrew Pearson was allowed to go with him.

There was an agonising wait, as everyone hung around to see who the victim was. The train had to stay right back, and no one was allowed to get off whilst the track was cleared. Finally it chugged into the station, all the passengers looking pale and wan.

'It was dreadful,' said Miss Cartwright, who had been shopping in Shrewsbury. She was held up by Colonel Trent, who had also been on the train. Another door opened and a very handsome young soldier got off. Peg did a double take.

'Tom? Tom Yeardley?'

'Hello, Miss Bradbourne.'

'Frank!' Peg called along the platform, without ceremony. 'Frank, he's here. Tom is here!'

Frank Yeardley, Constable Archer and Doctor Pearson had started their walk back along the track. When Frank heard his name, he looked up. His walk became a run when he saw his son. He bounded up the platform like a man twenty years younger.

'My boy,' he cried, when he reached

Tom. 'My boy!' He hugged his son, then put his hand around the back of his neck, pressing Tom's forehead against his. 'Don't ever do that to me again, you hear?' As if only just realising what Tom was wearing, he stepped back. 'What have you done?'

'I've joined the army, Dad. I needed to get away, but I didn't want to go without saying goodbye to you.'

'Oh you idiot! You didn't have to join up. They've not brought conscription in yet. Why, Tom? Why? Isn't it enough that your brother is out there? Do I have to lie awake at nights worried about you too?'

'I have to do my duty, Dad. Besides, I ... I can't stay here, not with him bothering me all the time. He won't leave me alone, Dad. I thought if I joined the army, I'd learn to be braver.'

'Who, son? Who's been bothering you?'

'Percy Fletcher,' said Peg, cutting in. 'He's been bullying you, hasn't he, Tom?'

'Well he won't be doing that anymore,' said Archer, who had caught up with Frank. Pearson was looking grim.

'What do you mean?' asked Tom.

'We've just found him, lad,' said Archer. 'It looks very much like he threw himself onto the tracks.'

Tom's knees almost buckled in shock. Frank had to catch him. 'Well, now you don't have to go,' said Frank.

'I can't get out of it now, Dad. I've taken the king's shilling.' Whilst the practice of pressganging young men to join the army had long since ended, it was still accepted that once a soldier had received his first week's pay, he was in the army and could not get out of the contract.

'Oh, son . . . I'll buy you out. I've got some money.'

'No, Dad. I've got to go. I want to go. I leave tomorrow, so let's not argue about it anymore.'

Frank and Tom left the station together, talking earnestly.

'Poor lad,' said Gerry. 'More bloody cannon fodder.'

'Let's hope it doesn't come to that,' said Peg, thinking of her brother Freddie. Pushing away the dark thoughts, she looked at her watch. 'Oh, look at the time. I'd best get back for lunch. Miss

Harrington? Cassie?' She turned to see that Cassie was in deep conversation with a woman dressed all in black.

'Oh, Miss Bradbourne . . . Peg.' Cassie turned and gave her a dazzling smile, yet there was something harsh and brittle behind it. 'Would you believe my mother was on the train? Mother, I'd like to introduce you to Aunt Veronica's step-daughter, Peg Bradbourne. Peg, this is my mother, Penelope Harrington.'

'I'm very pleased to meet you,' said Peg, holding out a hand. The hand offered to hers was icy cold, despite the warm day. The woman's dark eyes were not much warmer.

'And you, Miss Bradbourne. Cassie tells me that we're staying with you.'

'Oh,' said Cassie, looking flustered. 'I only said that I'd ask if we could both stay, Mother.'

'That's not what you said at all, Cassie,' Mrs Harrington snapped. 'Really, girl, your memory is getting worse. She's rather useless, Miss Bradbourne, but I have to put up with her, especially now I'm a poor widow.'

'You are both welcome to stay with us,' Peg said levelly. For the first time she stopped resenting Cassie Harrington and began to feel deeply sorry for the girl.

'Then I suppose that will have to do,' said Mrs Harrington. 'Come along, Cassie. Let's not keep Miss Bradbourne waiting. It's been bad enough waiting on the train because some selfish person decided to jump in front of it.'

As they walked from the station, with Peg having invited Gerry Sanderson to lunch, they passed the Quiet Woman. Frank and Tom were standing outside in the sunshine, both nursing a pint. It seemed to Peg that it was Frank's way of treating his son like an adult. The scene brought a lump to her throat. She had watched Tom Yeardley grow up. Would she one day be saying prayers for him in church, along with all the other young men that the village had lost?

Frank looked up and nodded his head slightly to Peg in acknowledgement. Then he saw Penelope Harrington, and his face became quizzical. He whispered something to Tom, who also looked at Cassie's mother. He nodded to his father, his brow furrowing in confusion. Peg was dying to know what they were saying and thinking, but Mrs Harrington forged forward, presumably remembering the village and where she was supposed to be going. She only stopped when Peg and Gerry pointed to the car in the square.

12

Lunch was a difficult affair that even Sheila and Mary's good graces could not rescue. Peg wanted to be at the station, finding out more about Percy Fletcher and what had made him take his own life. Peg believed that Percy thought too much of himself for that. In her opinion, there was too much suicide going around. Three people in less than a fortnight? It did not make sense.

The company at lunch did not help. Mrs Harrington had a way of finding fault without actually saying anything. Unless she was speaking to Cassie.

'Your hair needs pinning,' Mrs Harrington said, just as Cassie started to eat her soup. Mrs Harrington scooped some soup onto her spoon then let it go, as if testing the consistency and finding it wanting. She sighed, impatiently. 'Go and repair it now, Cassandra.'

'Yes, mother.'

Then when Cassie sat down again, looking as if she had been crying, Mrs Harrington said, 'Oh, good lord girl, your nose is all shiny now. Go and put some powder on it.'

Cassie, who had shone like the sun when she first arrived in Midchester, began to fade and shrink before Peg's eyes. Young Mary, who absorbed people's emotions like a sponge, looked close to tears herself. Seeing the portrait of her mother had not helped. Rather than comfort Mary, it had only reminded her of her loss.

Peg remembered the height markings for baby Cassie on the nursery wall of the old doctor's house and wondered again who had done them. It could not have been the dour woman sitting at their lunch table. She took no pride in her daughter at all. Perhaps it was Doctor Harrington, and that was why he killed himself there, but that did not fit with what Cassie had said about neither of her parents taking that much interest in her. Peg wondered if it had indeed been a nanny, or Frank's sister-in-law, Tilly, and that had been Doctor Harrington's connection to that room.

'Sadly she hasn't inherited my looks,' said Mrs Harrington, when Cassie had left to powder her nose. It was clear that Mrs Harrington had once been a very attractive woman, but her lips were pursed and surrounded by tiny lines, and she had lines on her forehead, suggesting that she frowned a lot. Something about Mrs Harrington's obvious earlier beauty made Peg wonder, but she could not put her finger on what it was. Something she had heard.

'I think Cassie is very beautiful,' said Mary. Peg wanted to hug her.

'Yes, we all think so,' said Peg, realising the irony of her saying that after resenting Cassie for so long. But it suited Peg's contrary nature to disagree with the awful Mrs Harrington. 'Don't we, Sheila?'

'She's a peach of a girl,' said Sheila. 'Doctor Pearson thinks so.'

'And so do I,' said Gerry Sanderson, looking at Peg briefly as if to see if it made her angry. It did not. She thanked him for his support with a smile.

'Humph,' said Mrs Harrington. 'She'll be lucky if she does as well as a doctor, let alone a young man inheriting a fortune and a great hall.'

There was no answer to that, not even from Peg who should have been happy to hear it both from the point of view of Gerry and Andrew Pearson. Instead it made her sad. When Cassie returned to the room, Peg cast a sympathetic glance, but regretted it when Cassie looked as if she might cry.

The rest of luncheon was an ordeal to be got through, but somehow they managed it. Gerry made his excuses as soon as he could, returning to Bedlington Hall.

'Is there anywhere you would like to walk, for old time's sake, Mrs Harrington?' asked Peg. Sheila and Mary had returned to the school for the afternoon session. They were in the drawing room, drinking coffee and sitting in awkward silence. Peg remembered after dinner coffee with Veronica, and it had never been this dull, even if they disagreed on things. Funny how she missed her stepmother now that she was gone. She was hit with another pang of regret for all the mistakes she had made in regard to her stepmother.

'Not really. I barely know Midchester.'

'But you grew up here, did you not?'

'Yes, of course I did, but it's been over twenty years since I came here. I had no great love for the place, even then.'

'When is your husband's funeral?' Peg was really asking how soon she could get rid of this dreadful woman.

'That's something Mother and I need to sort out,' said Cassie. 'So if you don't think us rude, Peg, I think I'll take mother to the undertakers.'

'Of course I don't mind. If you need any help, Cassie, do ask for it.' Peg was inclined to be kinder to the girl now.

Cassie got up from her seat and then reached over and kissed Peg's cheek. 'Thank you so much,' she whispered. Peg felt the girl's wet lashes touch her cheek.

Mother and daughter left together. Peg watched them from the window. As soon as they thought they were out of earshot, they started to talk to each other.

Whatever they were saying it was very heated. Peg wished she could follow and listen, and was just considering doing so when the telephone rang.

'*Hello, Miss Bradbourne?*'

'Yes?'

'*This is Alexander Marshall. I was just clearing out my studio and I realised that your stepmother had forgotten some things from our last session. She left the robe she was wearing.*'

'Oh, it doesn't matter, Mr Marshall. I can't see me wearing it, can you?'

She was not comforted by the sound of him scoffing. '*Fair enough, but I thought your sister Mary would like the blue lapis lazuli brooch it was fixed with.*'

13

Peg looked at the two brooches side by side and realised that whilst they looked very similar from a distance, up close one was clearly star-shaped whilst the other, which was found at the hotel in Shrewsbury, was shaped like a flower, with a lighter blue stone in the centre.

She looked at the clock. It was too soon for Mary and Sheila to return from the school, but she needed to ask them if Veronica did own both brooches. Somehow she doubted it, as her stepmother had been something of a slave to fashion within her limited means, and it was unlikely she would own two of the same item, even if they were slightly different shapes.

But what did it mean if one of the brooches was not Veronica's? Very little as far as Peg could work out. She left Mary's room, where the brooch had been amongst the little girl's box of treasures, and went to Veronica's. Uncertain what she was looking for, she went through Veronica's own hoard of treasures, which were in the bottom drawer of her dressing table: dance cards, postcards, letters from Cassie, flowers pressed between the pages of a book of love poetry that had been a present from a beau called Ronald in 1899, and some grainy photographs of two young girls just into their teens, both dressed in white with a flower pinned on their chests. Veronica and Penelope Hardwick. Veronica had been very beautiful, even from a young age, with luxurious curls, whereas Penelope, who was several years older, had been plain, with lank fair hair. But there had also been sweetness in the dreamy half-smile that played on her lips. What had changed that sweetness into the hard-faced woman who gave birth to Cassie?

Peg looked at the photograph more closely as if it would give her the answer, but the quality was not good and it was hard to see either woman in the two girls. No, that was not strictly true. Veronica had matured, but still had that recognisable beauty. The answer was there, just out of Peg's reach, but she could not quite grasp it; and just when she thought she had worked it out, the telephone in the hall rang.

She ran downstairs, just catching it in time.

'Miss Bradbourne?'

'Yes — is that you, Frank?'

'It is, lass. Have you seen Bert Archer since he was at the station? I need to speak to him, but he's nowhere around. It's our Tom, Miss Bradbourne. I'm frightened . . . I . . . '

Peg heard a dull thump and a groan. 'Frank? Frank? Mr Yeardley?'

With an icy finger of dread running down her spine, Peg flew out of the house and ran all the way to the Quiet Woman, stopping to knock on Doctor Pearson's door as she did.

'What is it, Miss Bradbourne?' When Pearson answered the door, he had a napkin in his shirt as if he were taking a late lunch.

'Something's happened to Frank Yeardley. Come quickly.'

As Peg was not the sort of girl to have

wild fancies, Pearson did not need telling twice. He grabbed his jacket and followed her.

The pub was closed up at the front, but that was not unusual. Frank only opened all day on market days.

Peg ran around to the back door, which was slightly ajar. 'Frank,' she called, as she entered. Feeling a little foolish, she wondered if she had overreacted. Frank might have just dropped the telephone. But her instincts told her otherwise. The sound she had heard was one of pain.

They found him in the back hallway of the living quarters, lying on the floor, with the phone swinging from its cord. Peg put it back on the cradle, whilst Pearson tended to Frank.

'Is he . . . ' Peg swallowed hard, trying not to cry.

'He's alive,' said Pearson. 'But he's been hit on the head. There may be a fracture. We'll get him up to Bedlington Hall. It's nearer than the cottage hospital and I don't want to risk him having a brain bleed. Where is Tom?'

'I don't know,' Peg replied. 'But Frank

said something about being worried about him.' She paused, hardly able to bring herself to say it, but she had to ask. 'Doctor Pearson, is there any chance that Percy Fletcher's death wasn't suicide?'

'Are you saying that you think Tom pushed him onto the tracks?'

'Maybe. I don't know. Tom isn't here now, is he?'

'Let's sort Frank out, and then we'll worry about that. He may well be able to tell us himself. Telephone Bedlington Hall and ask them to send an ambulance down immediately. The chief physician there owes me a few favours.'

They waited for the ambulance, and as they did, Peg had a look around. A picture on the hallway wall showed two young women. Peg recognised one of the girls as Frank's wife, Milly. Milly and Tilly Blake had been very much alike. More so than Veronica and Penelope . . .

Pearson went with Frank in the ambulance, but Peg had to walk up to Bedlington Hall. It took her about twenty minutes to get there. When she did she saw Pearson outside, in deep conversation with Constable Archer.

'You're here,' she said accusingly. 'Frank was looking for you.'

'I'm afraid I've been rather busy, Miss Bradbourne.'

'Yes, of course, I'm sorry. I . . . ' Peg stopped as the door to Bedlington Hall opened and two police officers came out with Gerry Sanderson between them. His face was grim and defeated.

'What's going on?' she asked. 'Gerry, what's happening?'

'I'm sorry to tell you, Miss Bradbourne, that the man you know as Gerry Sanderson has been arrested,' Archer said.

'But he couldn't be the killer. He couldn't be . . . ' Peg felt the world around her collapse, along with all her silly little dreams.

'Mr Harry Carter,' said Archer, in official tones. 'You are under arrest . . . '

★　★　★

They let her in to see him later that night, after the police had questioned her for hours.

158

'We're just holding him until the military arrive, miss,' Archer told her. 'Then they'll deal with him.' He opened the cell door. 'You have a visitor, Mr Carter.'

'Hello, Peg,' said Gerry.

'Hello, Gerry.' She still could not get used to thinking of him as Harry Carter.

He smirked. 'Better call me Harry now.'

Peg sat down. She should have hated him, but she could not bring herself to do so. 'Just tell me why,' she said. 'No. Start with how.'

'We were travelling back from the front together, me and the real Gerry Sanderson. He told me all about Bedlington Hall, and all about his inheritance and the mother who would not claim it, but how he planned to as soon as the war was over. He had never been here, didn't know anyone, but he wanted Bedlington Hall.'

'Were you friends?'

'Hardly. It's like I said to you — war makes strange bedfellows. I was the camp thief. The one they relied on to beg, steal or borrow the things they lacked. But

159

none of them would have invited me home to meet Mother. I was useful to them when they needed it. No more, no less.'

'Did you kill Gerry Sanderson?' Peg asked. 'Did Veronica and Percy Fletcher find out about it? Is that why you killed them?'

'I haven't killed anyone, Peg. You have to believe that. The ambulance crashed on the way back, just as I said it did. The real Gerry Sanderson and the crew died. I was lying there for ages before anyone came along. It gave me time to think. Your cousin and I had both taken shrapnel in the leg, so all I had to do was swap his papers for mine. I was born in a bad part of London, but in my . . . career . . . I've pretended to be all types. The impoverished heir to a huge stately home was no real stretch. But I didn't kill anyone.'

'How did they find out the truth?'

'They brought in someone from our regiment earlier today, and he knew straight away who I was. I could have killed him, but I didn't. I always planned to tell the truth if it came out. I'd say I was shell-shocked or something and didn't know who I was. But I suppose I became too comfortable, being with you. I started to really believe I could do this. My only regret would be leaving you behind when I emigrated. That was my plan, you see. Sell everything and then disappear to where nobody knew me. Would you have come with me? Even if I'd told you?'

Peg's heart said yes, but her conscience demanded otherwise. 'No. Because you were so scathing the other day about people who inherited money, making out they were useless and hadn't earned it. But you didn't earn any of it either, Gerry . . . or Harry . . . or whatever your name is. You just thought you'd take it and I don't believe for one minute that I entered the equation.' Peg stood up, with as much dignity as she could muster. 'A man like you doesn't go for a girl like me. You just played me along, as the doting cousin. That's all.'

'You're the best thing about this place, Peg, and don't let anyone tell you any different.'

'Why should I believe you? You're a liar

and a thief.' The pain in his eyes when she spoke so harshly seemed real.

'Yes, that's what I am,' he said bitterly. 'Harry: good for a bit of tobacco or some coffee, but not quite good enough for the great niece of a grand old lady.'

A tear rolled down Peg's check. 'Oh, you bloody idiot,' she said, before she fled the room sobbing.

She walked around Midchester until it was starting to get dark, struggling to get her emotions in check. She believed Gerry — Harry — when he said he had not killed anyone. He was an opportunist thief but not a killer. Or perhaps she was just deluding herself.

Over and over again, she replayed his words in her head. Something he had said had resonated, but then she lost it. She walked up to the railway bridge that Percy Fletcher was said to have jumped off. There was a path leading down from it to another path straight into the station.

Peg stared at that path for a long time before the truth hit her. When the train had pulled in and people milled around, it was hard to see who got on and who got off. Someone could have easily walked down to the stationary train and jumped into an empty carriage, lost in the confusion of the accident.

She ran down to the train station along that same pathway and spoke to the porter. 'Did Tom Yeardley catch a train back out of Midchester today?' she asked.

'Yes, Miss Bradbourne. I've just told Constable Archer that.'

'And Tom definitely got on the train?'

'Oh yes, miss. Definitely. His dad saw him off. Right upset young Tom were, but Mr Yeardley insisted.'

'Frank wasn't frightened because Tom is dangerous,' she muttered to herself. 'He was frightened because he thinks Tom is in danger!'

14

Before going to the old surgery, Peg called in on Miss Cartwright. The old lady rambled, but hidden amongst her gossip was the truth of the matter. Arthur Harrington had wooed her, thinking she had money, but dropped her as soon as he realised she was impoverished. He had then turned his attentions to the simple but sweet Penelope Hardwick. They had married and had a little girl called Cassie, but Harrington had been unable to contain his wandering eye. Vampish Tilly Blake, who had her own daughter, Helen, had been Harrington's last known affair in Midchester before he and his wife moved away to 'start again'.

On her way to the old surgery, Peg called back at the police station and asked them to send Constable Archer along as soon as possible. 'Tell him to bring a man and a shovel,' she said, satisfied that his disbelieving expression turned to one of shock. She asked if she could borrow a lantern and a shovel of her own and was given both.

It was getting dark, but Peg would not be swayed in her purpose. She ignored the front door of the house, knowing that there was no way through there to where she wanted to be. Around the back, the window to the room that was used as the surgery was broken. She climbed in, ripping her slacks on a nail.

She held the lantern aloft. As she had suspected, both doors had been nailed tightly shut. That had not stopped those who broke in through the window looking for any drugs that Doctor Harrington might have left. Whatever there might have been had gone. Only a few dirty bandages and other dressings lay strewn on the floor.

Whereas the rest of the house had wooden flooring, the floor in that room was made up of stone slabs, because it had once been an old outhouse that had been extended to create the surgery. The stones shone under her lantern like sacred tombs. Peg shivered. If she was right, that was what they were.

She prised one stone up with the shovel, her work on Bedlington Farm giving her more strength than most young ladies. It took a bit more effort to move it aside, but she managed to do so. By the time she had moved three of the stones, there was a tap on the inner door. 'Miss Bradbourne? Peg?'

'Constable Archer! You'll have to come around and through the window. The door is sealed.'

A few minutes later he joined her in the surgery room, accompanied by a young constable. 'What is going on?' he asked.

'Help me to dig and then I'll tell you,' she said, her mouth set in a grim line.

Archer was about to protest but seemed to think better of it. 'Okay, Peg. I know you and I know you're not given to idle fancies.'

It was late in the night when they found what they were looking for: two bodies, one adult and one child.

'God bless them,' Peg said, falling to her knees.

In the early hours, Peg let Archer and

the young constable into her house. They had called for Doctor Pearson on the way and filled him in on what had happened.

When Peg opened the front door, Sheila came to the top of the stairs. 'Peg, darling, we were getting worried about you. Whatever has happened?'

'Bring . . . Mrs Harrington . . . and her daughter down here, Sheila, please. But don't wake Mary. I don't want her to hear this.'

Sheila did not need telling twice. She brought the two women to the drawing room, where Constable Archer looked out at the early morning light and Pearson stood in front of the fireplace, trying to gain some warmth from the dying embers. The young constable had been told to wait outside the front door, whilst the back door had been locked securely. The key was in Peg's pocket.

'What is going on?' asked Mrs Harrington. Cassie's eyes were bigger than ever.

'Peg?' said Constable Archer, without turning. 'This is your show. Why don't you tell your story?'

'It seemed to me there have been too

many sisters mentioned lately,' said Peg. 'Pretty sisters and plain sisters. Gentle, loving sisters and bad-tempered sisters. Veronica and Penelope Hardwick and Milly and Tilly Blake — sisters with money; sisters without money; wives and mistresses. There have been too many suicides too. Oh the first one was definitely a suicide. Doctor Harrington did blow his own brains out, and in the room where his daughter spent most of her short life.'

'I don't follow you,' said Cassie.

Peg noticed that Andrew's eyes lit up. 'Of course you don't. I've said that all the way here,' he said to her. 'How could you know?'

'She didn't,' said Peg. 'But I think she does now. Don't you, Cassie? You saw it as a way to earn your freedom from your mother.'

'I don't know what you mean,' said Cassie, her eyes downcast.

'It seems none of us do,' said Mrs Harrington. 'Sheila, is your sister often given to flights of fancy?'

'No, not at all,' said Sheila. 'Peg is the

straightest person I know.' She smiled at her sister. 'But I wish you'd explain yourself, dearest.'

'Years ago, it was rumoured that the man I shall call 'Uncle Hardwick' favoured Penelope Hardwick, and left her an annuity. He left nothing to Veronica. Veronica always wondered why, and so did others. Was there some nefarious reason behind his taking care of Penelope but not her sister? Actually there wasn't. That was just a vile rumour put around along with the equally vile rumour that Penelope Harrington was cruel to her daughter. She was not. She adored her daughter, happily charting the child's growth on the nursery wall.'

'I'm glad to hear you say it,' said Mrs Harrington, raising an eyebrow.

Peg scoffed. 'Penelope was a plain girl, whereas Veronica was beautiful. But Penelope also lacked something. She was not as bright intellectually as her beautiful sister. So I think, though I don't know for sure, that Uncle Hardwick decided that Veronica would always be all right. She was beautiful enough to find a well-to-do husband. She almost married a young man called Ronald, whom she loved desperately. But I think he must have died in the Boer War. So she settled for father and security. And she was a good wife to him, even though I've denied it all these years. Penelope also married well. To a doctor. It must have surprised Uncle Hardwick, but he probably thought she was safe as long as no one else could gain from her annuity. Unfortunately she married a man with a wandering eye. Arthur Harrington had an affair with Tilly Blake, Frank Yeardley's sister-in-law. They had a very public break-up in the town square, but things weren't really over, were they?' Peg stared hard at Mrs Harrington.

'I forgave Arthur for that. Of course I did.'

Ignoring her, Peg said, 'The annuity Uncle Hardwick left to Penelope was only for her lifetime. But Doctor Harrington was tired of his wife and not doing so well as a doctor. Miss Cartwright told me that. People didn't much like his bedside manner. Anyway, where was I? Yes, he broke off his affair with Tilly Blake, who wrote to her sister, Milly, from Southampton or Portsmouth or somewhere in that area, saying she had found work and was taking her daughter, Helen, with her.'

'My friend,' Cassie said, gruffly.

Peg looked at her sharply. 'Then Doctor Harrington, with his wife and his young daughter, emigrated to America, where they have lived for the past twenty-odd years. Tilly Blake seemed to disappear off the map completely. Tonight — last night — we went to the old surgery and dug for hours. Constable Archer, do you want to tell them what we found?'

'We found two skeletons, an adult female and a child.'

'No!' Sheila put her hands to her face. 'How awful.'

'We can't say for certain, but they've probably been there about twenty years or more,' Archer explained.

'So are you suggesting my husband killed Tilly Blake and her child?' asked Mrs Harrington.

'No, that's not what I'm suggesting at all,' said Peg. She turned to Cassie. 'You know it isn't. You remembered, didn't you? When you saw the brooch?'

'What brooch?' asked Mrs Harrington. Her hand flew instinctively to her chest. For the first time she looked worried.

'The one you dropped at the hotel in Shrewsbury when you killed Veronica. But it's not the exact same brooch as Veronica's. Mary knew that too, which was why she was confused when she saw it. There were two brooches, one for each sister. At least that was the intention. That's why Cassie dropped her tea cup. She knew it was the one you wore constantly.'

'You have no proof of that,' said Mrs Harrington.

Peg would not be thwarted. 'You met Veronica at the hotel, perhaps with some promise that you'd help her out of her current financial crisis, and then you killed her, because you thought she was the only person in Midchester who could definitely say that you were not her sister, Penelope.'

'Ridiculous! Cassie, tell her who I am.'

'The reason Cassie has written to her

and not you,' Peg continued, 'is because she would know her sister's writing. I'm sure the manager of the hotel will remember you too. Constable Archer, is he on his way?' Peg prayed that Archer would play along.

'Oh yes, he should be able to identify the lady easily enough.'

Mrs Harrington went to make a move toward the door, but Sheila blocked it. 'Peg,' she said. 'Sweetheart, I'm confused. If it's not Tilly and Helen Blake up at the old surgery, who is it?'

'The people we found buried were Penelope and Cassie Harrington. This woman is Tilly Blake, and the girl we know as Cassie is Helen Blake.'

15

'Preposterous!' Mrs Harrington turned fiery eyes at Peg. 'You have no proof. As you point out, Veronica is dead.'

'We will know when Frank Yeardley wakes up. And if that fails, there's a photograph at the pub that proves it. You and Milly were more alike than Veronica and Penelope ever were. Others might have forgotten Penelope Harrington and how she looked, especially after a twenty-year gap, but Frank had his wife's face before him for a good fifteen years, even growing older, reminding him exactly how you looked.'

'You're mistaken,' Mrs Harrington protested. 'Completely mistaken.'

'Stop it,' said Cassie. 'It's over.'

'You knew?' Andrew Pearson started. 'You knew she had killed Veronica and tried to kill Frank?'

'That's not all,' said Cassie. 'She killed the boy too. Percy Fletcher.'

'Shut up!' Mrs Harrington went as if to hit Cassie but was stopped by Archer.

Cassie continued, 'He had Father's suicide note that told everything as you've detailed it, Peg, and he was blackmailing Mother with it. For years I thought Helen was another person, but when I went up the old house I began to realise the truth. It was Penelope Harrington who was kind to me when my own mother was not. I remember now how gentle she could be. She might have been slow, but her heart was that of an angel.'

'Why didn't you come forward when you found out?' asked Pearson.

'I thought that I'd be free of her,' said Cassie. 'If she knew that I knew, I could use it to escape her.'

'You mean like Veronica escaped, and like Percy escaped,' said Peg.

'I had to believe that if she did not kill me all those years ago, she would not kill me now. I had to believe that there was some tenderness in her for me.'

Mrs Harrington — Tilly Blake — scoffed. 'You stupid girl. We took you because you were the more pliable — the stupid one.

There was no way the real Cassie would have accepted me as her mother, but you . . . you latched onto any man I brought home as your father.'

Cassie fell to her knees, sobbing. 'Do you see how it is?' she asked Andrew Pearson. 'Do you see why I hid the truth?'

He shook his head. 'No, I'm sorry, I don't. Because of her, young Mary upstairs is motherless and the Fletchers have lost two sons. If you'd told the truth, you'd be free because she'd be locked up. Don't you see that?'

'But Andrew, the annuity would have stopped and I'd have had no money. I have no skills. I could not have survived.'

'Peg manages it,' he said. Any other time, that would have thrilled Peg, but whereas Andrew was without sympathy for Cassie, she felt some. The girl had spent all her life being told she was useless. It was very hard to move on from that.

'Are you going to tell them about Frank Yeardley?' her mother asked, a malicious smile playing on her lips.

'You said it was all I had to do to be

free!' Cassie cried.

'You hurt Frank?' Peg looked at her incredulously. 'But he was your uncle. He cared about you. His wife cared about you! Tom is your cousin. They would have helped you.'

'They have no money,' said Cassie, a coldness creeping into her voice.

'You really are your mother's daughter,' Peg said. For some reason she felt disappointed. She had hoped that Cassie would turn out to be one of the victims in all this. She supposed blood would out. But even that could not be right, because Tom Yeardley was a good, honest boy.

Archer called for the constable, who had been joined by other men as per Archer's instructions. 'Take them both away,' he said.

'Andrew,' said Cassie, gazing at him with limpid blue eyes as they put handcuffs on her. 'Please, help me.'

16

'Why don't you start taking your things up to your room, darling?' Peg said to Mary. She looked around the hallway of the old constable's cottage. It looked much brighter with a fresh lick of paint. She opened the door to the sitting room, which had also been decorated. There was still much to do and Peg had spoken to a builder about extending the house. They had turned the old jail cell into a larder, but Peg wanted a larger sitting room and another bedroom, just in case Sheila did decide to live with them.

'Can't Izzy do it? I want to go and look in the garden.'

'I've told you, dearest, that Izzy can only come in for a few hours a week. I can't afford to pay her any more. We're going to have to start doing things for ourselves now.'

'Very well.'

Mary picked up a box and slumped up the stairs.

'Are you all right?' Peg asked. 'Really all right, I mean?'

Mary put the box down and turned around. 'I am now that I know Mummy didn't leave me. I knew she wouldn't. Though I'm still sad she's gone. And Sheila.'

'But Sheila will come back and see us, sweetheart.'

Norman, along with thousands of other young men, had been injured in the Battle of the Somme. Sheila had rushed to the southern hospital where he had been taken, and had written to say that they would marry down there and then move to Sheffield as soon as he was well.

'And Freddie.'

'Hopefully Freddie will return to us one day.'

'Why does everyone leave?' Mary asked, her little face wan. 'You won't leave me, will you, Peg?'

'No, I will never leave you.'

'If you want some of Mummy's money from the house to pay Izzy . . .'

'No. That's for you, for when you grow up. I have enough money for what we need until then. But we'll just have to do without the things we don't need. Do you understand?'

Mary nodded. 'We'll be very happy here, won't we?'

'Yes, of course. And you'll be able to go and visit Sheila in Sheffield whenever you want. When you get fed up of me.'

With the resilience of youth Mary laughed, stood up, turned back around and bounded up the stairs with her box. Peg heaved a big sigh. She had no idea how to bring up a ten-year-old girl, but she would do her best.

Feeling a wave of sadness rush over her, she looked around for something to do. There was plenty, with boxes strewn in the hall, but where to start? She had been working on emptying a box full of crockery for a while when Izzy arrived.

'I just thought I'd come to give you a hand,' she said.

'Izzy, I can't afford to pay you any more hours.'

'I don't want any money, Miss Bradbourne. I'm here to help. So let me.'

'Thank you.' Peg blew her a kiss. 'You're an angel.'

They worked together happily. Every now and then, Mary came down for another box. The last time, she stood in the doorway of the sitting room, looking nervous. She had something behind her back.

'What is it, darling?' asked Peg.

'I want to ask something.'

'Go on then!' Peg smiled.

'Can I put this picture of Mummy and Aunt Penelope — the real Aunt Penelope — on the mantelpiece? I know you didn't always like Mummy . . . ' Mary held out the photograph which she had put into a wooden frame she had decorated with shells from a trip to the seaside.

'Yes,' said Peg emphatically. 'Yes, we will put it there.' Peg took it from her and put it in pride of place on the mantelpiece. The sisters stood wrapped in each other's arms, looking at it. 'Veronica and I didn't always get on, darling, but she did leave me a very precious gift.'

'What's that?'

'Not what — who.' Peg touched the end of Mary's nose with her fingertip. 'She left you.'

A few hours later, the packing had been finished and Mary was in bed fast asleep.

'Izzy?' Peg asked hesitantly as they sat in the kitchen drinking tea.

'Yes, Miss Bradbourne?'

'I wonder if you'd mind staying for on an hour to look after Mary. I will pay you for your time.'

'You go on, Miss Bradbourne. We'll argue over money when it comes time for my wages.'

Peg put on her coat and went out into the autumn evening. She walked along Spinsters' Row, conscious of the curtains twitching as the elderly ladies sat at their windows, drinking a sherry and tutting about the modern world and a young woman who dared to go out alone at night.

A soldier was walking up the road towards her, but he was almost abreast with her before she realised who it was.

'Doctor Pearson?'

'Hello, Miss Bradbourne. I was just coming to bid you farewell.'

'You're joining up? But why? You're needed here.'

'I'm needed on the front, where young

men are dying through lack of rapid medical care.'

'Can I say nothing to change your mind? I don't want you to go. So many don't come back . . . '

'Oh I'll probably be miles from the front in a medical tent, so don't worry about me.' A train tooted in the distance. 'I'd better be off. Take care of yourself, Peg.'

The use of her name in such a tender manner was almost too much to bear. He reached down and kissed her on the cheek.

'You too, Andrew,' she whispered. 'God bless you.'

The Quiet Woman pub seemed bathed in a warm glow when she reached it. She went into the ladies' lounge, having no gentleman to accompany her into the bar, but it was not in Peg's nature to hide away in a corner. She pulled a tall stool up to the bar and perched on it.

A young man turned around, wincing slightly. 'Miss Bradbourne!'

'Hello, Tom. I'm so glad to see you home again.'

'They let me out because of this.' He

pointed to his leg. 'And to take care of Dad.'

'How is Frank?'

'Better every day, thanks. He doesn't remember much about what happened, or even that my aunty Tilly had come back to Midchester pretending to be Mrs Harrington, but he remembers me and our George and that's all that matters to me. Anyway, what can I get you? On the house.'

'No, Tom . . . ' Peg thought she might cry. So many people had been so kind to her when she had often been abrupt and tactless.

'If you hadn't found Dad he might have died. I owe you at least one drink, probably more.'

'In that case I'll have a bottle of stout, please.'

Tom raised an eyebrow. 'Stout?' His look said that it was hardly a lady's drink.

'My old nanny used to give it to me because I was anaemic as a child. Got a bit of a taste for it.'

Tom grinned and gave her what she asked for.

'You'll be wanting help, won't you?' she said to him when he returned.

'Yes, I reckon. Especially in the evenings when it's busy.'

'No need. I'll do a couple of evenings a week if you want me to.' Peg quickly estimated that even if she paid Izzy a bit for babysitting, she'd still have extra money to spare.

'You?'

'I'm sure I could learn how to pull a pint, Tom.'

'But you're a well-born lady, Miss Bradbourne.'

'I'm someone who needs a job desperately.'

Tom nodded. 'Okay, come in tomorrow at six o'clock and we'll see how it goes, shall we?' Even a short time in the army had changed him. Gone was the gangly, awkward youth with the innocent eyes. His eyes now spoke of a man who had seen too much and had had to grow up too quickly, and he had made a decision about giving Peg a job without dithering. Tom Yeardley was going to be all right.

'Thanks, Tom. I'll just enjoy my last

night of freedom, shall I?'

From the stool in the snug, Peg had a view of the whole pub and everyone who came and went.

She allowed herself a satisfied smile. It was much better than peeking out at the world through net curtains whilst nursing a lonely sherry.

THE END